NEW YORK TIMES BESTSE[illegible]

A K[illegible]

A WOLF'S HUNGER

DEDICATION

Quite simply for readers everywhere. For those of you who get lost in a story, in words, and truly enjoy any author's work. Thank you.

Also, to a dear friend, Monica La Porta. Not only is she an amazing author but she always has time to help others. Thank you for helping me make Rafe better with your critique, and more importantly, for your friendship, which I cherish.

Table of Contents

Chapter 1

The huge, black Wolf rushed through the forest driven by one thought stampeding through his mind: satisfy the abnormal hunger that overwhelmed him.

Despite his size, he hardly made a sound as he pursued his prey. The scent of a deer his only focus as he leaped over bushes, darted around trees, and zeroed in on his quarry. Although he had ravaged several animals already, more than enough to quench his appetite three times over, this hunger was different. It burned his belly with the constant need for more.

Rafe couldn't understand what was going on. He'd never felt such hunger before and his beast was almost insane in its quest for food. He'd tried to stop it after the first few kills, but the deep craving inside him pushed him onwards.

His Beta, Jacy, ran with him and Rafe could sense his unease. His Beta had no idea what was wrong with his Alpha and it unsettled the serious man, and his beast. Rafe could offer no explanation and that fact alone caused his own worry to escalate.

Never before had he felt so out of control and, as Alpha, that wasn't a good sign. He was always in command of himself, man and Wolf, so this was new to him too. He only hoped that when he finally sank his razor-sharp teeth into the elusive deer that this feeling of starvation would abate.

Although, the more he thought about it, he guessed not.

He'd been eating constantly for the past few days. His mother astonished at how much he'd managed to pack away, even for him, the amounts he was devouring were astronomical and if it didn't stop, he'd be forced to consult the Pack's Healer to find out what was going on.

That was for tomorrow, or the next day, because today all he could think of was the deer he chased. His Wolf almost howled with glee when he caught a glimpse of it up ahead, but he managed to overrule that thought. What would be the point of letting his prey know he was so close just so it could escape him, again?

Not happening, he thought as his pace slowed, dropping to slink along the forest floor. His massive paws sank into the leaves littering the ground, his body as close to them as possible as he sneaked along, ever closer to his target.

Jacy's Wolf joined him, his Beta nudging his side as his anxiety grew. Rafe could smell it on his friend, rolling toward him in great waves as he tried to figure out what was wrong with his Alpha.

Rafe ignored him, his only focus on the deer just a few feet away.

His Wolf was eager but he managed to keep control and slowly slithered forward under cover of the bushes. Only when he was barely two feet away, upwind of the skittish deer, did he launch toward it, landing on its back and bringing it down as his jaws clamped around its neck. As blood ran down his throat he sank his teeth in further, snapping the neck with ease.

The deer collapsed beneath him and his beast immediately started tearing great chunks from the dead animal, chewing quickly and swallowing even faster before continuing. A low growl warned Jacy to stay clear. This kill was his and he wasn't in the mood for sharing.

Jacy's brown Wolf paraded around him as he fed, his tail swishing back and forth, clearly indicating how upset he was. Tough. Rafe was hungry and he didn't need to ask permission from his Beta to hunt and feed.

An Alpha didn't answer to anyone.

The deer didn't last long, his Wolf devouring it in no time at all, but Rafe was shocked to realize he still felt hunger gnawing in his belly. What the hell was going on? A full deer to himself should have filled him up for days, but he barely felt as if he'd fed at all.

Finally his Beta encroached on his space, nudging him with his snout as he spoke through the Pack-link. *"Rafe, we need to go. It's morning. We've been out all night and we have to head back."*

"Morning?" Rafe asked, shocked as he looked up, the sun gleaming down through the treetops.

"Yes," Jacy answered. *"And when we get back we have to talk."*

Rafe didn't respond, knowing what he wanted to talk about and he had no answers for him. Fuck,

Rafe had none for himself either. He didn't know what the hell was going on and knew he'd been neglecting his duties as Alpha. None of that seemed to matter though. This hunger inside him needed feeding and that was the fact of the matter. That he didn't know what was happening to him was pushed to the back of his mind as he hunted.

Jacy was going to force his Alpha face what was going on and that annoyed the hell out of him.

His Wolf growled a low rumble deep in his chest before turning for home and speeding through the forest. Jacy kept pace. Never allowing his Alpha to get ahead, sticking close and making sure Rafe did not disappear.

"Damn," Rafe thought as he plowed through the underbrush with speed. He definitely was not looking forward to the conversation Jacy was obviously hell-bent on having.

He pushed the impending talk from his mind, instead reveling in the feel of allowing his beast free rein in the place he loved the most. The area around their camp was his haven, where he went when Alpha duties weighed him down. His love of nature ran deep in his veins and if he weren't Alpha, he'd spend far more time running wild and free.

However, he *was* Alpha and that position held responsibilities he sometimes felt weighed like a ton of bricks on his shoulders. He never allowed that to show, always calm and in control, and thinking of the Pack first.

As smoke from the camp filled his nostrils he slowed his pace, loping along the outskirts until he stopped at the back door of his cabin. The smell of his mother's cooking wafting toward him as he transformed, leaving his Wolf behind as the man appeared.

He'd changed so many times that he no longer felt pain or heard the sounds of his body realigning. His skin shivered against the coolness of dawn as he grabbed his jeans off the back porch, tugging them up over his thick thighs, and striding inside the warmth of the kitchen.

"Hey, you." His mom, Ellie, turned from the stove, spatula in hand, as she cooked his breakfast. "Where have you been this early?"

Rafe didn't answer immediately, giving Jacy the opportunity to enlighten her. "We've been out all night, hunting."

His mom moved the pan from the stove then turned back to lock eyes with him. Rafe stared right back as she raised an eyebrow, her tone questioning. "And what did you bring back?"

"Nothing," Jacy answered again, Rafe ignoring him completely as his mother nodded slowly.

"So you two won't want breakfast then?"

Jacy stepped around Rafe, heading to the huge wooden table. "I'm starving, Ellie. *I* didn't eat anything."

"Is that so?" Ellie said as she served Jacy a large plate of food.

"Yes." Jacy smirked as he glared at Rafe.

"Traitor," Rafe flung out through their link.

Jacy turned, his dark eyes locking with Rafe's as he shrugged. "Rafe and I have something to discuss, after breakfast of course."

"Honey,"—his mom pointed to the table—"come sit down and eat."

"Thanks." Rafe strode over, giving Jacy the evil-eye as he sat down.

A plate, piled high with food landed before him, then his mom sat down next to him. Too late Rafe realized she also wanted to talk.

"This has been going on for a few days, son, and I think I know what's happening."

Jacy stopped shoveling food into his mouth.

"Really? What's going on with him?"

Rafe huffed, interrupting. "Him? I'm *him* now. Whatever happened to showing your Alpha some respect?"

Ellie waggled a finger at her son. "Rafe, don't be an ass."

"I see," Rafe grouched. "I'm an ass now too. Great."

"Ellie," Jacy carried on, ignoring his Alpha. "What do you think is wrong with Rafe? I'm worried about him. You know he actually growled at me while he hogged an entire deer?"

"What?" Ellie's eyes popped open. "He ate an entire deer on his own?"

"That wasn't all," Jacy replied, his voice lowering conspiratorially. "He'd already had three kills before the deer."

"Enough!" Rafe slammed down his cutlery. "Stop talking as if I'm not even in the room!"

Jacy slowly returned his cutlery to the table before turning to glare at Rafe. "Maybe if you'd discuss the problem we wouldn't have to."

Nobody else would get away with speaking to Rafe like that. Not if they wanted to stay in one piece and if there were other Pack members around, Jacy wouldn't either. In the confines of his cabin though, the normal rules relaxed. It was the only way for his Beta to call him out on things that he needed to.

Those times were rare, but they did happen and Rafe exhaled loudly before looking into his best friend's face. "All right, I admit that there's something going on with me, but I don't know what the fuck is going on!"

Ellie shook her head. "Language," she chastised. "Rafe, you look like hell, and your appetite is out of control. So, do you want me to tell you what I think is wrong? Or are you going to continue snapping at everyone and acting like an idiot?"

"Go on." Rafe waved his hand at his mom, not at all sure he wanted to hear what she had to say.

"This is something I've heard about before, this hunger you have." Ellie reached over, patting his hand reassuringly. "I know you can't control it and you've been in Wolf form far more than usual. There's a reason for that."

Ellie paused when Jacy sat forward, his tone incredulous. "You *know* what's wrong with him? Why didn't you say anything before? I've been worried sick about him."

Rafe snapped at his Beta. "You've been

worried in case you need to take over for a while."

Jacy's face flushed at being caught out. Rafe knew he hated when he had to run the Pack if he were away. His friend blustered, trying to cover his true feelings. "No, no, I admit I don't particularly like being in charge, but I honestly have been worried for you."

"Will you two boys stop bickering like toddlers," Ellie said in exasperation. "If you'd hold your tongues I could possibly get this finished before lunch."

Jacy snorted as Rafe held up his hands in defeat. "Go on, Mother."

"As I was saying." Ellie's face sobered, her tone as serious as Rafe had ever heard it. "There are old legends that speak of such a thing. Where a Wolf's Hunger takes over control and . . ."

Rafe sat forward, spearing his mom with a glare. "You *know* these so-called legends to be true? Or are they just stories with nothing to back them up?"

"Don't use that tone with me. I know you're upset about what's going on inside you, but I'm certain that I have the answer. That's if you'd stop interrupting."

Jacy interceded, ever the peacemaker. "Hey, you two, come on, let's all calm down."

"I'm perfectly calm," Rafe lied as he sat back, crossing his arms.

"Darling." Ellie tilted her head, staring hard at him. "I can feel it inside you. It's gnawing away at you and you *have* to listen to me or you'll end up going insane."

Jacy couldn't help himself. "As in really insane? Or is that just a euphemism?"

Ellie threw her hands up in the air, exhaling loudly in exasperation. "Right! That's enough. I don't want either of you to say one more word until I've finished."

She looked at Jacy who ran his fingers across his lips as if zipping them, Rafe merely nodded. "All right. The legend has been spot on so far, with the hunger that's inside you, and your beast being more and more in control. Am I right or am I right?"

Jacy nodded but Rafe didn't respond, refusing to admit to anything so Ellie sighed, carrying on. "I know I'm right, Son, you don't have to say one word. I'm your mother and I can sense things that others can't."

"Will you just spit it out?" Rafe ground out, the

hunger inside him taking hold again.

"You have to go and find someone," his mom whispered.

"What are you talking about? Find who?" Rafe blurted out, annoyed at his mother's cryptic words.

"She'll be somewhere near, Son, but you need to go and seek her out. She . . ."

"She who?" Rafe shook his head. "Mom, you're rambling."

Ellie looked at Jacy then back at her son, her face defiant as she dropped the bombshell. "Your mate. The hunger is a sign your mate is near and she needs you."

Jacy looked dumbstruck as Rafe jumped up, his chair toppling over as he glowered down at his mom. "Don't be ridiculous. I don't want a mate. I don't *need* a mate."

His mother looked up at him, determination in her eyes. "Son, you may not want one but you do *need* one and if you don't find her soon, you'll be lost to the hunger for goodness knows how long. I've heard that it can actually drive a man insane. So please, listen to me and go and find her."

Rafe shook his head, denial running through him like hot lava. "You're wrong."

Jacy stood and looked about to say something so Rafe about turned and left, heading back to the forest to unleash his Wolf.

CHAPTER 2

Jacy stared open-mouthed as Rafe disappeared. "Ellie, are you sure about this?"

"Yes," Ellie rose, wringing her hands with worry. "Jacy Runningwolf, you are Beta of this Pack and it's your duty to make that hard-headed son of mine see sense. If you don't, I fear for him, and the Pack."

"How can you be so sure though?" Jacy prodded.

"I just am," Ellie scowled at the Beta. "I mean it. It's your responsibility to get him to go and find his mate. If he doesn't then he'll be no use to anyone and we might lose him forever to his beast."

"That serious, huh?" Jacy asked quietly.

"Yes," Ellie replied, her face white with worry. "Please, go and try to talk some sense into him."

"I'll do my best," Jacy headed out, pausing at the door to look at his Alpha's tense mother. "I'll have to make a quick stop to get Levi to take over for me and I'll let Ali know too. She's always wanted more responsibility and this is as good a time as any."

"Thank you," Ellie said with relief.

"I'll make him see sense if it's the last thing I do." Jacy stopped, running a hand through his hair. "And with the mood he's in it very well might be the last thing I do."

"He has to see sense," Ellie said firmly. "He is Alpha and the Pack needs him. I'm sure that he'll know that when the time comes."

"I just hope that he realizes it before ripping my head off." Jacy said, shrugging. "I've got a feeling this isn't going to be easy."

"Nothing that's worth a damn is ever easy," Ellie said firmly. "Wait, how's your father? I know you went to see him last week but I've not had the chance to ask you."

Jacy shook his head sadly. "Still mad at Mom for not marrying him and he hasn't got over the fact I'm Wolf."

Ellie's eyes softened. "Your mother did the right thing, honey. Your father wasn't her mate and things would've ended badly. She could never have lived with him and, well, if he doesn't accept you for what you are . . ."

"You mean not a full-blood Native American," Jacy answered angrily.

"There's that plus the fact you're Wolf," Ellie replied fondly. "But look how far you've come within the Pack. You're Beta and that's something to be proud of."

"I am proud of being Rafe's Beta but my father doesn't seem to understand."

"I'm sorry, honey." Ellie walked over, patting Jacy's shoulder. "You belong here, with the Pack, and your mom loves you, no matter what."

"I know." Jacy nodded, his eyes still sad.

"You've got an important mission to do right now." Ellie raised an eyebrow. "Now scoot."

"I'm going," Jacy retorted, his feet moving slowly out of the cabin. "Damn, I hope he's calmed down by the time I reach him."

"What? Who?" Alinka, or Ali as they all called her, asked as Jacy came around the side of the cabin. "What's up? You look worried, Jacy."

"No," Jacy said far too quickly, Ali's eyebrows raising as she stared hard at him. "I've just got a lot to do and I was just coming to find you. Can you take over scheduling our Sentries? I might be out of camp for a while and want to ensure that's taken care of."

Ali broke into a huge smile, her short hair framing her face making her look far younger than she truly was. "Are you serious? Of course I will."

"Yes, I'm serious, now go and get things organized." Jacy watched as she spun away excited. "Wait, have you seen Levi?"

"Yeah," Ali flung over her shoulder, not slowing down as she sped away. "He's over at the Healer's, she wants him to go find some plants for her to use. You know he's the best at that."

"Thanks." Jacy headed toward the other side of camp, moments later finding Levi as he left their Healer's cabin.

"Morning," Levi greeted Jacy, his blonde curly hair a mess, as usual, his hand tucking some stray locks behind his ear. "You need me for something? I've got a list here from . . ."

Jacy didn't have time so cut him off. "I need you to take over for a bit. Rafe and I have something we need to attend to."

"Sure." Levi's face grew serious. "Can I help?"

"No, we've got it covered, but if you can take care of things here, I'd appreciate it."

"All right." Levi frowned, his blue eyes piercing him as he sized Jacy up. "Anything I need to be worried about?"

"No," Jacy lied easily. "Everything's all right."

"Okay," Levi replied, his stare following Jacy as he walked toward the forest.

He didn't like lying to his friend but there was no point in worrying anyone, and if Levi was thinking about Rafe then his mind wouldn't be on the job at hand. Taking care of the Pack came first so Jacy didn't enlighten him. He knew Levi was aware of the lie. The scent of it had hung between them, but Levi knew better than to press him. If Jacy was holding something back then that was his right as Beta, and Levi knew the rule: obey.

As soon as he entered the trees, Jacy undressed, wrapping his clothes in a bundle and hanging them from a branch. His transformation was quick, not as quick as Rafe's, but then again, nobody could transform like the Alpha. He heard his bones break, moving within his body to take the form of his dark brown Wolf.

Once the shifting was completed he shook his body, the fur rippling as he raised his head and sniffed. Catching the scent of his Alpha, Jacy took off at a fast pace, hoping against hope that he could talk some sense into Rafe.

He was under no illusions that it would be easy. Rafe could be hard-headed and stubborn, but if Ellie was telling the truth, Jacy had no option but to force his Alpha to go in search of the mate that his mother was certain was near.

"Good luck with that," he told himself as his beast loped through the forest silently.

Tasha jogged deeper into the woods, her pursuers not as far behind her as she'd thought, chastising herself softly. "Lazy bones, you shouldn't have slept so long."

She was exhausted, the "long" sleep had lasted all of four hours and she felt as if she'd been on the run for weeks. In truth it hadn't even been two, had it? No, it was barely nine or ten days but it seemed so much longer. Her heart ached as her mind filled with visions of her parents being slaughtered. They were so weak when the rogues attacked that they didn't stand a chance. The mysterious illness that ravaged her Pack was something none of them had witnessed before and nobody knew how to combat it.

As the illness struck, their Alpha had done everything he could, working with their Healers to help those struck down. Only a few weren't affected and Tasha was one of those. Her mother said she was "blessed" and "lucky" not to have fallen to the illness but Tasha felt anything but.

She nursed her parents as best she could, for five whole days, as they grew weaker and weaker. Then the rogues arrived.

A group of only twenty or so but it was enough to decimate her beloved Pack.

With even the Alpha lying sick in his bed, the rogues had swarmed through the camp, picking off her friends as they went. She'd grabbed her father's shotgun, standing guard at their bedroom door, waiting for the end to come.

She wasn't stupid. Tasha knew she'd die but she'd have the pleasure of taking at least a couple with her. Then her mom had to go and spoil her plans for a big exit, making her grab some clothes and sneak out the back and into the forest.

Damn! She'd fought her mother until her mom did something Tasha had never witnessed before: she cried.

Her mother actually cried. Shoot. How could she argue with her when she did that? She couldn't.

Tasha had grabbed some clothes, water, and a few precious items, stuffing them into a backpack and handing over the shotgun to her mom. The twisted smile her mother gave her tore at her heart and she swore she could hear it break inside her.

"Mom!" she'd implored. "Please don't make me do this."

"Tasha Montgomery! You'll do as you're told, missy." Her mom's voice was strong again, holding that air of command she used whenever Tasha didn't want to do something. "Not only do I need to know you're alive. You, my darling, have to warn other Packs. There's something not right about any of this and I'm scared to think that this is just the beginning. Others could be in danger, baby, it's your duty to alert them to what happened here."

Tasha's eyes blurred with tears as her mom reached for her, giving her one last kiss before ordering her to run. "Run as fast as you can and get the hell away from here. Live for me, baby, please."

She kissed her mom's cheek, then her unconscious father's, and sneaked out as quietly as she could. The rogues were near, in the very next cabin, as Tasha slipped into the dense trees. She'd barely ran a hundred yards when she heard the first loud boom of the shotgun, quickly followed by another, then nothing.

Her hand flew to her mouth to stifle the scream that almost erupted from her throat. Fury and fear fighting for pole position inside her. Her Wolf urged her on and she doubted she would've escaped if not for her beast. It pressed her onward when all she wanted to do was curl up and die.

Tasha was stubborn, and full of rage, so she pressed on, running away from her home and those she loved. She didn't stop for two days and it was when she woke on the third that she heard them behind her. They must've found her tracks and been on her tail ever since.

She wasn't sure how many were trailing her but it was more than a couple. Sometimes their voices reached her enhanced ears and she could make out at least four or five distinct tones. Tasha knew she wouldn't have a chance against that many and cursed herself for not thinking to bring her handgun with her.

A Wolf with a gun? Yeah, Tasha was a crack-shot and sometimes competed in competitions, that was until her dad found out. He'd given her hell for entering human matches, telling her she was cheating because of her enhanced abilities.

Tasha knew that was right, but she hadn't done it to win the prizes. She just liked the thrill of seeing how well she could do.

With everything that had been going on, she'd forgot the dang thing. If she hadn't, she might've been tempted to stalk her pursuers and see if she could take a few out. One bullet to the brain would do it. Nothing less would kill a Wolf but she was the best in the Pack with a handgun and she was sure she could've pulled it off.

"Stupid, stupid," she berated herself as she thought of the gun lying around doing nothing as she fought to survive.

At least she wasn't starving. The area she was in now was prolific with wildlife, and she hunted every chance she got. In her Wolf form, she'd just gobble her kill down, no need for cooking. That was one way of keeping one step ahead of the rogues on her tail. No fire, no smoke, so they couldn't quite hone in on where she was.

They were doing it the old fashioned way, tracking her, and Tasha was managing to stay ahead of them. Until now. Now they were right behind her and she had to get her ass in gear or they'd catch her.

She shivered as she jogged, the thought of their hands on her almost causing her to throw up. Tasha didn't want to think about what a group of rogues would do to her if they caught her.

Her long auburn hair flew around her head as she picked up speed but she didn't slow to tie it up. She didn't even have time to pee and she desperately needed to.

"Don't think about it," she whispered to herself, wishing she could stop and cross her legs.

"Come on, Tash, move!"

Tasha jerked. Those last words weren't hers. She hadn't said those and the urgency and tone were just as if her mother was right next to her, urging her on. "Mom?" she muttered, tears suddenly filling her eyes.

Silence. No more words of encouragement and the only thing she could hear were the rogues in the distance. Tasha drew a deep breath in, forcing her legs to move faster as she ran through an area she didn't know, scared she'd lose track of where she was going and end up running smack bang into those who chased her.

"Stop it," she rebuked herself again. "One foot in front of the other and keep going."

She tried to figure things out, again, wondering about the illness that had decimated her Pack, and just how did the rogues know when to attack? There was more to this than she knew but in order to get to the bottom of things there was one thing she had to do: survive.

Tasha knew there was a Pack in the area, she'd heard about it from the Beta when he'd been sent to do some business for her Alpha. She wasn't exactly sure where they were but it was in this general direction. She hoped she'd come across them soon so she could alert them to the threat, and they could also take care of the asswipes behind her.

That was the plan anyway.

If she survived long enough and didn't get caught. "Not happening," she told herself firmly as she continued on.

Tasha pushed all thoughts of her parents, and her Pack, from her mind, focusing on her escape and allowing herself to dream of seeing the rogues behind her getting ripped apart. Now *that* would be justice.

CHAPTER 3

Rafe ran swiftly through the trees, the scent of prey invading every pore of his Wolf body. His massive paws eating up the distance between him and his quarry. One thought alone spinning around in his head: hunger.

Jacy was behind him, not near enough for him to care, his beast leaving his Beta to trail after him as it raced after more food. More, more, more!

Rafe knew things were getting out of hand, subconsciously, but he didn't seem able to stop. His Wolf craved prey and he couldn't get it back under control. He pounced high into the air, landing on the back of a coyote, making quick work of ripping its throat out.

As soon as it lay dead beneath him his beast tore into it, ravenous as bloodlust flew through him.

When he'd devoured his kill he raised his head, Jacy standing in human form watching him closely.

"Alpha!" Jacy held up his hands in front of him. "We need to talk."

Rafe shook his head, black fur rippling over his beast but his Beta wasn't giving up.

"Alpha, change so we can talk."

Reluctantly Rafe transformed, scowling at his friend. "What?"

Jacy stepped closer, his eyes full of concern as Rafe paced back and forth. "Do you know how many that is? Or how long we've been out here, away from the Pack?"

Rafe stopped, shaking his head. "No."

"That,"—Jacy nodded to the bloody remains on the forest floor—"is your tenth kill in the past two days."

"Can't be," Rafe denied.

"It is," Jacy confirmed. "We've been away from camp for more than forty-eight hours, Rafe. This has to stop and you need to do what your mother told you. It's either that or you'll no longer be Alpha. A Pack needs their Alpha there, present, dealing with stuff, not running around like a wild animal for days on end."

Jacy stepped back, his body tensing as if he expected Rafe to attack.

Rafe admitted he felt like punching his friend, his hands clenching into fists at his side. It was at that precise moment everything his Beta had said made it through the fog in his mind.

"Shit," Rafe spat out. "You're right. I've no idea what's going on."

"Yes, you do." Jacy stepped forward again, his friend's voice full of worry. "Your mom is certain about what's happening to you and after watching you these past two days, I agree with her. So, I guess you need to take heed, my friend. Either that or lose your Pack."

Rafe stopped, facing his best friend and Beta, emotions rolling through him that he'd never experienced before. His Wolf howled in his head, so loud his hands flew to his ears. "Shut up!" he scolded it. "I need to think."

"I'll stay quiet so long as you agree to think about this," Jacy said quietly.

"Not you," Rafe tried to explain. "My beast is acting nuts."

"Ya don't think?" Jacy said, sarcasm dripping from every word.

Rafe started pacing again. His Pack meant everything to him, nothing could stand in the way of his being a good Alpha, but he had to admit he'd been anything but for the past week. He could count on his fingers the hours he'd spent in camp and that wasn't how an Alpha should act. He knew that, deep down, but this damn hunger had taken over and now he had to regain control.

"How do I do it?" he asked his friend slowly.

"Not sure about that part. But I'd start with accepting what your mom said and get your beast on board."

"I'm not ready for a mate," Rafe admitted his innermost fear. "I wouldn't know how to treat one and what if she doesn't want me?"

"Don't be stupid," Jacy replied curtly. "A soul-mate is the one person made for us, the *only* person we can be happy with. If you find her then she'll want you as much as you want her. Simple."

Rafe glared at his friend, huffing out, "There's nothing *simple* about any of this."

"Stop being a misery guts," Jacy went over, slowly, gauging Rafe's reaction. The past couple of days he'd had to stay clear or his friend would snarl and snap at him. When Rafe gave him a small smile, Jacy thumped his back. "We'll do it together. Now, have a talk with that Wolf of yours and let's see if we can get started."

Rafe gave a curt nod then inhaled slowly before blowing the air out. *"Hey, do you know anything about our mate?"*

His Wolf howled again, stomping around in his head. *"Yes! Go, now!"*

Rafe sighed with relief. "Apparently my beast is on board."

Jacy grinned wildly. "Thank the gods for that."

A vision of a grey Wolf with a black bushy tail appeared in Rafe's head, his own beast circling around it. *"You know what she looks like? You could've let me in on this sooner."*

"Stubborn," his beast grumbled.

Rafe couldn't disagree, instead he apologized to his friend. "Sorry for being an ass."

Jacy's eyes widened in surprise. Rafe rarely, if ever, uttered those words. "I'd say that's okay, but really, it isn't. You've been so wrapped up in yourself this past while that you've been neglecting the Pack. You should know better, Rafe."

Pack was everything to Rafe and he couldn't believe he'd acted so out of character, so he let his Beta's comments slide. "Noted."

"Can we get on our way?" Jacy asked pointedly.

"Sure," Rafe said a moment before he transformed.

His massive beast waited for his Beta, Jacy's brown Wolf joining his moments later. Relief flooded Rafe as he realized the urge to hunt was subsiding. In its place was a deep need to find the grey beast he'd seen in his mind. That was the only thing he could think of as he raised his nose then took off through the woods.

~~~

Tasha paused at a stream cutting through the trees to quench her thirst. She'd been on the move for hours and was tiring. "No time," she told herself as she picked up her backpack and leaped nimbly over the small rivulet of water.

As soon as her feet touched the ground on the other side of the stream she gasped, all oxygen leaving her in a loud exhale as emotions flooded her system. Not only that, but a vision of an ebony Wolf
~~~

with grey tipped ears appeared in her head.

"What the hell?" Tasha shook her head to clear it. She couldn't slow down, those damn rogues seemed to be catching up to her and she had to move or be caught.

"Ours," her beast repeated over and over in her mind, confusing her about as much as it annoyed her.

"Not now!" she tried to shut it up. Tasha had to focus and her Wolf misbehaving right now was definitely not a good thing.

Her heart beat faster as she plowed on, visions of the black Wolf prancing with her grey one causing her to trip and fall forward. She barely managed to stop her face from being ripped by a nearby thorn bush. "Damn it, will you *stop*?"

Tasha implored her Wolf as she picked herself up, brushing herself down and trudging on. The sounds of voices nearby had her heart thudding with fear. She took off running, desperate to put some distance between her and the rogues on her tail.

"Shit," she cursed as her foot disappeared down a rabbit hole, her body tumbling to the ground, hard.

Pain exploded inside her ankle and she knew it was broken. She could feel bones scraping against each other as she tugged her foot free. Tasha crawled to a nearby tree, using the trunk to haul herself up, realizing she'd have to transform to heal herself.

She'd stayed in human form because of the large pack she carried. It held the locket her mother had given to her on her last birthday, a family heirloom that had been handed down for generations. There was also pictures of her parents, ones that she would never allow to be lost and if she transformed she would've had to leave the pack behind.

Her only saving grace so far was that her pursuers had not changed either. If they had she was certain they would've caught her days ago. Now it looked like she had no choice, her ankle hurt like a bitch and she *had* to get away.

If she didn't then her Pack would have died for nothing, and nobody would know what happened to them. Tasha couldn't allow that. No. Freaking. Way!

Dropping her pack, Tasha held onto the tree with one hand, attempting to get rid of her jacket with the other. Large fingers snatched hold of her hand resting on the tree, and she couldn't stop the surprised squeal that rang from her mouth. The arm belonging to the fingers was thick, strong and attached to a man that came into view as she tried to shake off his hold.

"Let me go!" She struggled hard. Her ankle gave way, and she plummeted to the ground as the rogue grinned evilly at her.

"Over here!" he shouted as she scrambled like a crab away from him.

"Shit," she mumbled, her head swinging left and right looking for his friends.

Tasha struggled to regain her footing, her toes the only thing that touched the ground on her damaged side. Even that was like hot lava running through her ankle as she limped away from the man closing in on her.

"You have nowhere to run," he snapped out, his disgusting breath causing her to gag.

"Well, well, what do we have here, boys?" A slimy voice had Tasha's head spinning around to see four more rogues closing in.

The man who spoke was the tallest and the look in his eyes told her he would show no mercy. Her blood rushed through her as her fight or flight went into overdrive. Neither of which was a good option, not with a broken ankle anyway.

"What is *wrong* with you?" Tasha spat out. "Why are you doing this?"

"Nothing is wrong with us, doll," the obvious leader drawled. "We're getting paid, plain and simple."

"What?" Tasha asked, shock reverberating through her. "To kill an entire Pack? Why?"

"Does it make any difference if you know?" the leader said harshly. "The outcome will be the same for you."

Tasha shook her head as his eyes narrowed, traveling up and down her body. Her insides churned at his look and she tried to put some weight on her ankle. If she could move maybe she'd have a chance.

Nope. Pain lanced through her, causing her to bite her lip to stop from yelling out.

"But first you're going to pay for making me and my men hunt you down." He licked his lips and that had Tasha almost throwing up. "What happens now is your own fucking fault. You should've just stayed put and it would've been over and done with nice and quick. Now, bitch, you're going to suffer."

"No!" Tasha screamed as they closed in. With no way out, she feverishly thought how she could end this as quickly as possible.

She'd rather die than have these men touch her.

Her knife! She'd kept it in her sheath at her

waist.

She wasn't stupid enough to think she could take these rogues on, but she could take her own life. Not something she'd ever thought about before. However, with these filthy mutts closing in on her, she knew it was the only way out. She could not, *would* not allow them to capture her and do unspeakable things to her. No. She refused to be yet another of their damn victims.

"I'm sorry, Mom," she whispered as she tugged the blade free.

CHAPTER 4

Rafe's Wolf sped through the forest, a sense of urgency deep inside him that told him he had to hurry. Their mate was in danger and he had to get to her, fast.

Jacy was behind him, struggling to keep pace with Rafe's beast, but that didn't slow him down. His Wolf urged him on, hurtling through the trees toward their mate. His blood boiled when he heard a scream, the sound reverberating through him as red hot fury spilled through him.

He was near, but would he be in time?

Another high pitched yell, full of anger and

fear, came through the woods, his Wolf full of desperation as he surged onward. As he broke through thick underbrush he took in the scene before him.

A young woman with long auburn hair stood, surrounded by five men who were closing in on her. Damn rogues!

Rafe could scent it on them as he slid to a silent stop, looking for the biggest threat to their mate. A tall man sneered at the girl, his words spearing Rafe's heart.

"What happens now is your own fucking fault. You should've just stayed put and it would've been over and done with nice and quick. Now, bitch, you're going to suffer."

The girl shouted, "No!" as the rogues closed in.

Rafe caught a glimpse of steel in her hand as he leaped past her, landing on the man who'd threatened his mate. His Wolf's powerful jaws locked onto the rogue's throat, ripping it to shreds before slashing his chest with his claws. His beast took no chances, shredding the man's torso in seconds and wrenching his still-beating heart free, dropping it on the ground and attacking the next threat.

He could hear Jacy's own attack. His Beta was ferocious when riled and Rafe knew he would show no mercy. Neither would he.

Rafe managed to kill two in human form before they had a chance to transform. When he turned around after his second kill, he came face to face with a huge brown beast. Its fangs snapped at him, a snarl erupting from its throat as it launched an attack. Rafe's powerful beast met it head on, soaring high to clash mid-air, teeth and claws meeting in a battle for the ultimate prize: life.

As soon as they met in battle, Rafe knew this rogue had had more than his fair share of fights. His dirty tactics were annoyingly nasty, but Rafe's beast dealt easily with everything thrown at him and soon the rogue lay dead in a pool of blood.

His head spun around, looking for the next threat. Jacy had killed two, one wolf, one in human-form, but the remaining rogue held his mate firmly in front of him, a shiny blade in his hand. His blood turning to ice in his veins.

The dirty scumbag held the knife against the pale white skin of her throat. Rafe stalked forward, snarling and pawing the ground in anger. The man shook his head, sneering.

"Stay there or she dies," the man spat out as his arm around her throat tightened.

"No," the girl, his mate, choked out. "Don't kill him, we need him to get information about . . ."

"Shut the fuck up!"

Rafe watched as the rogue grabbed her hair, tugging her head back violently and spitting into her face. The look of revulsion on her beautiful features causing his beast to go into a frenzy of bloodlust.

A roar of stifled fury tore through the forest, his beast shaking with pent-up anger. He lifted a front paw, slamming it down onto the ground, leaves and dirt spraying up as he tried to keep the rogue's attention fully on him. His Beta was limping, the rogue smirked as he watched Jacy finally fall to the ground and crawl away almost had Rafe attacking.

"Don't worry," Jacy spoke to him through their link but he barely heard the words as his Beta hauled himself away.

Rafe's beast paced back and forth, head swinging low and growling. "Stay there, mutt." The rogue sneered, tugging his mate against his body and forcing her to walk backwards.

A yelp of pain from her caused Rafe's heart to

physically ache for her and it was then he noticed how she held one of her feet. Only the toes touched the ground and she could not put any weight on it at all, hopping as the rogue used her body as a shield.

Her face was pale and drawn as she hissed through clenched teeth, pain obviously running through her. Seeing his mate suffer was like a knife to his heart as he paced.

"This is how it's going to go down," the man bit out, his eyes never leaving Rafe. "I'm going to leave and I'm taking her with me, as collateral, and if you follow us, then I'll slit her neck so quick you won't know it's happened until her blood soaks the earth. So, you mangy mutt, back off, now."

Rafe's fur rippled across his body at the mere thought of losing sight of his mate. Her eyes were wide as she locked onto his, hers were the most beautiful shade of grey he'd ever seen. She pleaded with him in that look and he knew he could not allow the rogue to take her.

But how was he going to rescue her without harm?

Jacy's voice almost gleeful as he whispered inside his head. *"Countdown begins . . . now. Get ready, Rafe."*

Rafe shook his head, trying to clear it and also look for his Beta. Where the hell was he? He'd looked badly injured as he'd crawled away.

"Three, two, one – go now!"

Jacy yelled through their link as he hurtled through the bushes behind the rogue, his jaws clamping onto the man's shoulder, the one attached to the arm holding the knife.

Rafe sprang forward, transforming mid-stride and snatching his mate from the arms of the fucker that held her captive. He picked her up, cradling her in his arms as Jacy pinned the rogue to the ground, his jaws at the man's neck.

"No!" the woman in his arms yelled, waving an arm around. "Don't kill him. We need him."

"Jacy, do as she says," Rafe ordered as she looked up into his face with thanks written all over her pale features.

"I'm Tasha and my Pack has been destroyed." She leaned her head against his shoulder. "We need to figure out what's going on or all Wolves could be in danger."

She gasped out the last words before falling into unconciousness. Rafe tightened his grip, holding her firmly against his naked body and fought not to take vengeance on the rogue lying bloodied before him.

"Jacy," Rafe ground out, jaw clenching and unwilling to utter the words he knew he must.

Jacy's head turned to Rafe, blood dripping from his jaws, his eyes questioning.

"He's our prisoner." Rafe shook his head in disgust. "Transform and escort him back to camp. I'll contact Levi and get him to send out some guards to help."

His beast moved off the rogue, nudging him to get up. When the man lay still, Jacy nipped his thigh.

"I suggest you do as you're told, otherwise my Beta will inflict a hell of a lot of pain on you but he will not incapacitate, or kill you. It's your choice."

Rafe didn't bother waiting to see what happened. Jacy was more than capable of dealing with the man so he started back to camp. Levi was shocked when Rafe spoke to him through their link but he was already on his way with two more Wolves to help Jacy.

Striding quickly through the forest with his mate in his arms, Rafe took the time to take in every detail. Her hair was a mess, dangling down over his arm and tickling his bare skin, it was filthy and bore testament of her time running from the rogues. Her words earlier causing sadness to seep into his soul.

An entire Pack killed?

That was outrageous and he'd make damn sure to do everything in his power to get to the bottom of what happened. The grief he felt inside her almost taking his breath away, and he guessed she'd lost loved ones. Rafe remembered too well how he'd felt when his father died. It was cataclysmic and the worst thing he'd ever experienced.

It had been unexpected. He was Alpha. Strong and fearless but something as simple as a drunk driver had ended his life. His mother barely hung on and it was through the grace of the Goddess that she'd survived. Her own grief at losing her soul-mate was the most horrendous thing Rafe had ever witnessed.

Days, weeks, and months passed in a blur as they all fought to keep his mom going. Her desire to just fade away was so great that Rafe thought on many occasions that he would lose her too.

Luckily, with the help of the Pack, she'd finally turned a corner. The first time Rafe saw her smile after that fateful day made his insides flutter and his heart rejoice.

What his mate had endured was far worse. Her entire Pack, everyone she knew and loved, had been snatched from her and Rafe knew she would need a lot of support to deal with that. No matter what it took, he'd make sure she recovered. She was his mate, his love, the center of his life from this moment on. Rafe could afford her nothing less than everything he had.

Her scent ingrained within him, deep down, as if it had always been there and he knew without a single doubt, that this woman was his.

Rafe stopped, on alert, when he heard Wolves heading his way. He'd been so lost in his own thoughts that they were almost upon him by the time he heard them. Sending out his Alpha power he recognized Levi and two guards stampeding toward him. Levi's massive light brown beast skidding on the wet leaves when he saw his Alpha.

"Jacy should be on his way, behind me, but I have to get her back to camp."

Rafe noted Levi's eyes widen as he inhaled, his beast's nostrils flaring at the change to his Alpha's scent.

"I'm sure you know what she is, but just to

enforce how important she is. I'll spell it out for you: She is my mate. Now, go and help your Beta and I'll want to see you at my cabin later. We have a problem with rogues."

The brown Wolf lowered its head, whining once then taking off with lightning speed. Levi was one of the quickest Wolves he knew, his pace so fast that few could keep up. The two guards he'd brought with him falling behind within seconds.

Rafe smiled as he pictured the rogue's face when Levi arrived. He was large, much bigger than most other Wolves, and he was an imposing and scary sight. When he wanted to be that is. It was one of the reasons Jacy and Rafe chose him to deal with the Pack guards and dole out punishment when it was due for minor infractions. Anything serious was dealt with by Rafe, or Jacy if he wasn't around, but they rarely had major problems within the Pack.

That may no longer be the case. Not if rogues had the power to take out an entire camp.

Rafe had to find out what happened and how to stop it. He refused to allow rogues to kill any of his people and he'd do whatever it took to ensure their safety.

He'd go so far as to call in the dreaded Council.

Rafe hated their rules and regulations but they had manpower behind them. If required, he'd go cap in hand and ask for their help.

Even if the thought made him want to puke.

Chapter 5

Rafe skirted the camp, not wishing to parade through it while holding his mate. His Wolf was jumpy and it definitely didn't want anyone near her.

No, that wasn't true. It didn't want any *males* near her.

He trudged up the back porch, hoping his mom was home. "Mother! I need your help."

Hearing her voice chatting before she replied. "I'm in here. What's got you so upset? If anyone should be upset it's me! You've been gone for . . ."

Her mouth fell open as Rafe strode through, Alinka's eyes dropping to the floor before popping back up to stare at the woman in his arms. "Mom, she's hurt and exhausted."

"Follow me." Ellie raced toward the stairs, ushering him up as she went up side-stepping so she could keep her eyes on him. "Who is she? What happened? And, Rafe, is that blood all over you?"

Rafe ignored her. His entire being focused on the woman in his arms. He'd realized earlier that she was younger than he'd first thought, probably early twenties, if that. It didn't make any difference to him, she was still his mate and Rafe would fight to the death to protect her.

He also realized he didn't want to put her down. His mom held the cover back on the bed and urged him to place her on it. Rafe couldn't help the growl that crept up his throat as he laid her gently down. The loss of her touch was a physical pain running through him.

"Rafe," Ellie said his name quietly, her hand on his arm. "Are you all right? Your scent has changed and, well, that usually means one thing."

Rafe's eyes locked with hers, nodding once he confirmed what she suspected. "She's mine and she's hurt. Plus, there's a problem with rogues. She said that her entire Pack was killed, Mom. Everyone. I think she's the only survivor."

"Oh no," Ellie gasped, a hand flying to her

heart, eyes wide and her face losing all color. "Where did this happen? We have to do something."

"I'm not sure," Rafe admitted. "She passed out before she could tell us anything else."

"Fuck!" Ali's curse had him spinning around.

"Ali, I need you to get as many sentries out as you can. We have to protect the Pack until I can gather more information."

Sure," she said, nodding quickly before disappearing.

"Jacy is on his way back with a prisoner," he said with loathing. "One of the rogues who'd cornered her. He's the only survivor. Jacy and I killed the others."

"That's something at least." Ellie went to work, inspecting the girl lying lifeless on the bed. "I hope you can get him to answer your questions."

"He'll have no choice," he said firmly. "I'll make sure he talks, no matter what it takes."

Ellie stood back from the bed, tugging the thick quilt over his mate. "Her ankle is broken and she's dehydrated and exhausted. Once she's up to it, if she transforms then her ankle will heal."

"I thought as much," Rafe agreed, having used his enhanced senses to feel out his mate's injuries on the walk home.

"I'll go and get a bowl and some warm water to give her a wash." Ellie waggled a finger at him. "You go shower and dress, then we'll talk some more about your mate."

Rafe growled, not wanting to leave his mate alone for even a second. He nodded to the attached bathroom. "I'll shower here, can you bring me some clothes, please?"

"Son, she'll be fine," his mother tried to coax him to leave.

"I said I'll shower here," Rafe replied firmly, his tone full of his Alpha power.

Ellie lowered her head as his power washed over her. "I'll be back soon."

Rafe felt a twinge of regret at using his power but then he shrugged, his attention back on the body lying in the bed. "What's your name?"

She didn't respond so he forced himself to go and clean up.

It was the quickest shower he'd ever had, washing himself quickly to get rid of the muck and blood. When he walked back into the bedroom, a towel wrapped around his waist, his mom was back.

She nodded to a chair. "There's some clothes

for you."

Rafe snatched them up, dressing quickly and taking a moment to apologize. "I'm sorry about earlier, Mom. I'm not quite myself right now."

Ellie turned, her knowing eyes gazing up at her son's. "I know that, honey, it's all right."

"How is she?" Rafe asked, coming to sit on the side of the bed, his hand reaching out to move strands of hair off his mate's face.

"She's resting," his mom told him as she started to wash his mate's face and hands. "She's gone through a lot, Rafe. She'll need our support to get through this."

"I know," Rafe whispered. "I just hope we can help her."

"You will," Ellie told him with a confidence he didn't feel. "Having her mate at her side will do far more for her than anything else."

"She's gorgeous, Mom," Rafe's voice hitched, full of emotion as he looked over at his mother. "The most beautiful thing I've ever laid eyes on and I don't even know her name."

"Tasha," a weak voice had them turning quickly to the bed. "My name is Tasha Montgomery."

"Well, hello, Tasha, my name is Ellie," his mom said quickly.

"You rescued me." Tasha's shaky voice tore at Rafe's heart.

"Yes," he said, smiling. "I'm Rafe Blackstone, Alpha of the Darkmoon Pack. You're here in my home and I promise to keep you safe, Tasha."

"You, you, shoot . . ." She stopped as recognition flamed in her eyes.

"I'm your mate, Tasha," Rafe confirmed.

"Oh." Tasha's eyes lowered, her face flushing red.

Rafe wanted nothing more than to hold her in his arms, brush his lips over hers, but he stayed in place. "It's a lot to take in. I know. I was shocked too but there's no mistake, Tasha."

"I know." She looked up through her long, dark lashes, her pale grey eyes searching for his. "I'm just a little . . . well . . . I'm not sure, stunned I think."

"We'll take things slowly," Rafe said the words he knew he'd find difficult to follow through on. Not when his body craved hers beneath him as she cried out in pleasure.

"Rafe." Tasha tried to sit up, her yelp of pain halting her. "Dang, my ankle, I fell and it hurts like hell."

"It's broken, dear," Ellie said, patting Tasha's arm. "Once you feel strong enough, you should transform and let it heal."

"I have to talk to you first," she said as her eyes found Rafe's again. "There's so much and I'm not sure where to start."

"I'd much rather you healed yourself before we do anything else," Rafe replied, his insides churning at the pain he could clearly feel she was in.

"No," she said firmly. "I have to tell you what happened to my Pack. It's gone, everyone is dead, and I have a feeling that we won't be the only ones."

Ellie brought a glass of fresh OJ over. "Here, drink this first."

Tasha snatched it, gulping the juice down quickly. "Thanks."

"I'll go and get some food while you two talk."

Rafe shuffled closer, taking one of Tasha's hands in his. The need to have a connection growing inside him with each passing second. "All right, tell me what happened."

Tasha gave him a sad smile, her fingers entwining with his. "An illness swept through the camp and nobody knew what it was, or how to get rid of it. Right at the beginning people tried to transform to heal themselves, but it didn't work, and then they had trouble changing back. It was horrendous watching it."

Tasha shivered at the memory, Rafe reaching out to run a finger down the side of her face. "I can't even imagine what that would be like."

"After the first few had such trouble, nobody else tried. It was obviously something our beasts couldn't heal." Tasha gulped, her eyes filling with tears. "My mom and dad got sick, in fact only a few of us didn't, but we're not sure why. I wasn't at the camp when the first people fell ill, so I think that had something to do with me not getting whatever it was."

"I'm grateful for that." Rafe squeezed her hand.

"I was too, at first," Tasha admitted sadly. "But watching everyone you care about become so ill was . . . unbearably horrific. I was powerless to help them and they just grew weaker and weaker. My dad was unconscious when the rogues arrived."

Rafe felt grief rolling off her, his instinct to protect her gnawing in his belly. "I lost my dad a few years ago. I remember how bad it felt."

Tasha looked up at him, her eyes full of sadness. "I guess it was a blessing, in a way. The rogues swept through the camp, killing everyone. I grabbed my dad's shotgun but my mom insisted I give it to her and leave. I argued. How the hell could I leave her?"

Tasha's voice broke, sobs tearing from her throat. Rafe moved quickly to sit next to her on the bed, pulling her into his arms. "Aww, baby, I'm so sorry, but your mom was right. If you didn't escape then how would anyone know what happened? Or get revenge for the atrocity?"

"I get that," Tasha mumbled into his chest. "But it was the hardest thing I've ever had to do. I shoved some things in my backpack and gave her the gun, then I ran. I'd barely gone a few hundred yards before I heard it go off. I got away by the skin of my teeth."

"Aww, baby, that must've been awful, especially hearing the gun." Rafe could only presume he knew what the sound must've meant for Tasha.

"It was." Tasha sniffled against him. "Mom wouldn't have fired until she was sure of hitting her target so I guess she managed to take at least one of them out. She was fiercely protective of us and with my dad unconscious next to her, she would've done anything she could to . . ."

Tasha obviously couldn't carry on, soft sobs escaping as he held her tight. "Shh, it's okay, you're safe now. I promise I won't let anyone hurt you."

Her head jerked back, her teary grey eyes staring into his. "You can't promise that, Rafe. Even our Alpha was sick, really ill, and nobody had the strength to take on the rogues. Most were in bed when they came, too weak to even get up."

"I'll do whatever it takes," Rafe said with conviction. "I need to know where your Pack was so I can go and check things out. I have a few mixed-Wolves in the Pack, several that are part Witch, so I'm hoping they can help uncover what happened. In fact, our Healer is magical so she should be in a good position to figure out what this mystery illness is. I'll also contact the Council, they can organize a clean-up of your camp and bury the dead."

"I need to be there for that," Tasha's voice hitched. "I have to say goodbye to my parents and everyone else."

"I'll make sure that it's safe first. I can't have you in danger, Tasha. You're too precious."

"Sorry." Tasha's eyes flashed with anger. "That

wasn't a request. I'm going and that's not something open for discussion."

Rafe was about to bite back a retort when his mother arrived. Her calming voice interrupting, "I've brought you something to eat. Rafe, she needs to rest, so why don't you go down and speak with Jacy, Levi, and the rest of the Wolves that are congregating outside. They are all upset and if you don't go and relieve Jacy then I think he's going to rip that man's head off."

"They're here?" Rafe stood, still holding one of Tasha's hands and loathe to let go.

"Yes, they need their Alpha, Son," Ellie replied softly. "Go and sort things and I'll help Tasha."

Tasha tugged her hand free, urging him to leave, which was the last thing he wanted to do. "Go, see if you can get any information out of the rogue. We need to know what's going on before we can tackle it."

Rafe knew he had to go but his Wolf howled loudly at leaving their mate, but he forced himself to stand. "I'll leave some sentries around the cabin, just in case."

"Thank you," Tasha replied. "Oh wait, do you know if my backpack was found? It's got stuff in it I don't want to lose: pictures of my parents and my mom's locket."

"I think it's downstairs," Ellie said as she passed over a plate piled high with food. "I'll get it in a minute."

Tasha merely nodded as her eyes stayed locked with Rafe's as he backed out of the room. His heart already hurting as he left.

This was a time when newly found mates should be spending every waking moment together, binding themselves to each other. Instead he left her and went to deal with his Pack. An Alpha's duties came before anything else, including this. There'd be time for him and his mate to get to know one another, to bond, to find ecstasy in each other's touch. Now was not that time.

Right now he needed to be the most bad-ass Alpha he'd ever been and deal with their prisoner. He'd show that damn rogue the power he held within and not blink an eye for any pain he inflicted.

Chapter 6

Jacy circled the rogue wearing jeans and nothing else. His dark skin glistening , his muscles rippling as he prodded the man. "Tell us what we want to know."

The bloodied and battered man merely snarled, a look of loathing on his face as he spat on the ground.

Levi was there with several of his men and a large group of the Pack stood watching. Their eyes wide and worried as their prisoner shouted. "You'll be dead soon enough. The whole fucking lot of you."

"I doubt that," Rafe drawled as he strode toward his Beta. "You get anything useful?"

"No," Jacy growled. "This fucker hasn't given

us anything."

"And I won't," the man sneered.

"Yet," Rafe said coldly before turning away. "Levi, I want guards on my cabin at all times. My mate is inside and she's the only one of her Pack to escape this scumbag and his friends. She is our top priority. Understand?"

Levi bowed his head. "Of course."

Rafe waited as Levi shouted out orders and half a dozen men broke away to circle the cabin. "Keep your wits about you."

"They will," Levi told him firmly.

"Now," Rafe said coldly, turning back to his Beta. "We'll deal with *him* in a minute."

"Sure," Jacy snarled at their prisoner. "I'm looking forward to it."

Rafe turned to the nervous crowd. "I'm sure you're all concerned about what's happened. The loss of a Pack is unheard of but I need you to stay calm. I'll be contacting the Council and I'm sure they'll get to the bottom of what's going on. In the meantime I want you to be careful and stay close to the camp. Ali's got sentries out and working to keep you all safe and I'll be going to see what I can find out as soon as I've finished with this scumbag."

He looked around, catching the Pack Healer's eye. "Myrtle, I'd like you to accompany me when I go."

Myrtle stepped forward. "I'll go and get my things ready."

"Tomorrow morning is soon enough," Rafe told her. "We'll leave at dawn."

"Okay," Myrtle replied, nodding. "Is there anything I can do for your mate? Is she hurt?"

"She has a broken ankle but that'll be fixed when she changes and her Wolf heals her." Rafe smiled at the small woman, her unruly blonde curls like a halo around her head. "Thanks for asking though."

"If you need me just let me know," Myrtle said before turning to leave then stopping and asking, "I assume you want my magical side tomorrow?"

"Indeed I do," Rafe confirmed. "I'll talk with you more in depth in the morning. For now, just prepare yourself to tap into that side."

"Will do." Myrtle's eyes hardened as she glanced at the rogue. "If you require my assistance with that piece of crap, just holler."

"I don't think that will be necessary." Rafe snarled toward the rogue. "I'm going to take great pleasure in dealing with him myself."

Myrtle smirked, her eyes twinkling with mischief as she left. Her tiny feet flitting across the ground as if she were dancing.

"Now, everyone else, just go about your daily business and let me deal with this situation."

Rafe watched as the crowd started to slowly dissipate, one after the other, leaving him and his Beta with the rogue.

He looked around, tapping his chin as he pondered on where to do the interrogation. Not an interview, not "questioning the suspect." Nope, this was going to be a full-on Alpha grilling and one he hoped would cause their prisoner a fair amount of pain.

His cabin was set back from the rest, but he wanted a more secluded spot to deal with this asshole. Rafe nodded to himself, settling on what he would do. His jaw set and his eyes hardened as he turned to Jacy. "Bring him."

Rafe strode away into the forest. They had a small cabin set in the woods to use when hunting for the Pack. It was quite some distance from the camp but that suited his requirements just fine. He planned on having the rogue roaring in pain and the farther they were from camp the better.

His booted feet stomped through the lush greenery, his mood darkening with each step. Rogues had murdered Tasha's parents, together with the entire Pack, but the grief he'd felt inside his mate caused his anger to rise to levels he didn't know he was capable of feeling. Rafe was normally cool, calm, and collected. Not today, not at this moment. Right now he wanted to rip something apart and his anger would be targeted toward one person.

Rafe wondered if he'd manage to contain his fury, or would it unleash and cause him to kill their only lead.

"No," he told himself as he carried on, his footfalls heavy and loud in the silence of the forest.

Jacy pushed and prodded the rogue, forcing him to follow Rafe. His Beta's own anger was boiling inside him, Rafe could feel it, and he knew, without a doubt, he'd never felt that in Jacy before.

"Guess destroying an entire Pack does that to a guy," Rafe thought as he plowed through bushes and anything else that stood in his way.

Any other day he'd take in the beauty all around him. He loved being in the forest, whether in human or Wolf form, but today he barely glanced at the magnificence of the area. His sole focus on garnering whatever information he could from their prisoner so he could pass it on to the Council.

Rafe was under no illusions now. They needed help. If there was someone, something, out there that could kill a Pack of Wolves, then Rafe would ask for help from anyone he could. Including the Council.

He smirked as he pictured the Council leader's face when Rafe called asking for help. He never contacted them for anything, so he was certain they'd be surprised when he called asking for assistance.

Atherton Denholm was old, even for a Wolf, but he ran the Wolf Council with a rod of iron. Although their rules and regulations annoyed the hell out of Rafe, he was well aware that Atherton would help any Pack in times of need, and this definitely counted as that. Rafe just didn't relish actually having the conversation.

He'd make it short. As short as possible. That way it would be over and done with and the Council could step in and help. After all, Rafe didn't look forward to going through a camp of dead Wolves and laying them to rest. Nope. That was definitely on his "absolutely never to do" list.

As he finished that thought, he saw the cabin in

the distance, throwing over his shoulder, "Nearly there."

Jacy appeared pleased, prodding the man in front of him and gleefully spitting out. "You hear that? Nearly at the place where you're going to have a world of hurt. I'm looking forward to this."

Rafe heard the hatred in his Beta's voice. He would have to be deaf not to. It didn't surprise him one bit. His Beta led his life devoted to the Pack and what these rogues had done was horrific. Neither Rafe, nor Jacy, could comprehend the destruction of an entire Pack, men, women, and kids. Outraged was how Rafe felt and he was pretty damn sure Jacy was too.

He'd have to ensure his Beta didn't lose it and kill this lowlife before they could get any answers. Hell, he needed to make sure *he* didn't kill the fucker.

Not until he got all he could from him. After that? It was a toss-up whether he'd tear him apart or hand him over to the Council.

Rafe was well aware of some of the punishments handed out by the Council. Having their beast ripped magically from them, or being forced to transform and magic used to keep them in Wolf form. Both of these were excruciatingly painful, and permanent.

Would it be a fate worse than death?

It would for Rafe but he wasn't so sure about the rogue. They didn't value what they were, what they should be part of. Apart from the pain inflicted, he doubted they'd care either way of the outcome.

"Rip him apart it is," Rafe said inside his head, his beast yipping with glee at the prospect.

Rafe pulled the door to the small cabin open. "Inside," he growled at the rogue who stumbled forward after a hefty push from Jacy.

"Tie him to the chair." Rafe rummaged around in a large wooden box, pulling out some rope they used to tie up larger kills.

"You think *that* will hold me?"

Rafe ignored the man as Jacy pulled out a chair from the table and pushed the rogue down roughly. His Beta went to work, binding the man's arms behind him but also to the chair, before bending to tie his ankles to the legs. When he stood, Rafe sent him a private message.

"Transform, your Wolf might come in handy."

Without a word, Jacy shrugged off his jeans and let loose his beast, the cabin suddenly feeling much smaller with his Wolf taking up so much space.

It snarled at their prisoner before heading behind him, pacing back and forth with growls rumbling from its chest.

Rafe sent another message. *"If he doesn't answer my questions, or if he's just being a dick, give him a few nips to remind him you're there."*

"With pleasure," Jacy replied, his voice full of loathing but tinged with excitement at being allowed to inflict some of his own punishment.

"Name?" Rafe demanded.

"Fuck you." The rogue sneered, his eyes full of disgust as he glared at Rafe.

"I said," Rafe ground out, opening up his Alpha power and allowing it to pour toward their prisoner, "*Name!*"

The man's eyes widened as pain lanced through his body and mind. The intense pain inflicted by the Alpha power invading his every pore and causing his face to pale, his teeth to grind together as he fought against it.

"I can up the stakes anytime." Rafe shrugged, sending a fraction more of his power toward the rogue. "I haven't even started in earnest yet so I suggest you answer."

Rafe rarely used this particular Alpha ability.

He hated to inflict pain of any kind, but the one doled out using his Alpha power was beyond cruel. Hence, he rarely utilized that part of him. For this rogue he'd make a damn exception.

"What difference does knowing my name make?" the rogue groaned out, his breathing ragged as he tried to fend off Rafe's power. "I can tell you and it won't make one jot of fucking difference so why don't you just get on with what you really want to know."

Rafe turned away, his anger boiling up inside him. He focused on the window, looking through it to the lush greenery outside. His forest, his land, his haven. It usually calmed his soul, taking in the beauty of the trees, bushes, animals that shared their homes with his Pack, but today all he felt was worry when he looked outside.

There was a threat to him, his people, his land, and he had to garner information to combat that peril.

"Very well," he said coldly, turning back to face the bloodied man. "Tell me what happened to Tasha's Pack?"

"Who's Tasha?" the rogue asked a moment before his eyes twinkled evilly. "Oh wait, is she that tasty bitch we caught earlier?"

Rafe held himself in check but Jacy nipped the rogue's thigh and the resulting yelp of pain caused Rafe to feel pleasure he didn't know he was capable of as he spat out. "Answer the question."

"All right!" The rogue's voice rose as Rafe sent another wave of his power to invade him.

"I'm not a patient man," Rafe advised, his tone cold as ice.

"First, you need to understand I'm not high up on the food chain, so to speak." The man raised an eyebrow toward Rafe. "The first guy you killed earlier, he would know more than me, that's for sure but I'll tell you what I do know."

Rafe crossed his arms and glowered at the man, sending another shockwave of power to keep him on track.

"Ouch! Will you stop that?"

Rafe merely shrugged, smirking.

"Okay, okay," the rogue said quickly. "Someone wants land, a lot of land, and they're prepared to go to any lengths to get it. I'm not sure how they made those Wolves sick, but we were told to wait for five days then go in and kill them all. Nobody was to be allowed to live, or leave."

Rafe's anger grew as the words spilled from the

rogue's mouth and he couldn't help himself from sending another, stronger wave toward the lowlife.

"Please!" he yelped, grinding teeth to withstand the pain running through him.

"How many of you were there?" Rafe asked quietly. He needed to know how many rogues they might have to deal with.

"There was about thirty of us but most of them left when everyone was dealt with. We knew one had escaped, so my boss, the guy you killed, his name was . . ."

"Irrelevant," Rafe spat out. "Go on."

"We tracked her until we caught up to her today." His eyes looked into Rafe's showing the lack of compassion held within.

"And you were going to play with her then kill her. Right?" Rafe asked, knowing the answer.

"Sure."

"Then what?"

"What?"

Rafe exhaled loudly, barely controlling himself as he snarled. "What were you to do after you'd taken care of her? Where were you to go? Who were you going to meet? What was your next job?"

"We were to meet up with the rest and wait on

word of where next to strike." He paused. "As I said, the big boss, whoever that is, wants land, as much as he can get and you know how he's going to get it. Take out anyone inhabiting what he wants. He's got the magic to do it and he obviously doesn't give a shit about a Pack of Wolves standing in his way."

"Shit!" Rafe growled, desperate to know who was behind this horror. "Tell me where you were meeting up with the rest of your rogues?"

"If I tell you will you let me go?" the man whined.

Rafe snorted, shaking his head. "No. You have two choices. I hand you over to the Council or I deal with you."

"But I've answered your questions! I was just following orders."

Jacy gave the man another nip, his resulting yell causing Rafe to smile. "You killed an entire Pack who were infected with god knows what but something that made them vulnerable and unable to defend themselves. You cannot understand how that makes me, as Alpha of my own Pack, feel. I swear to Mother Earth I want nothing more than to end you and nothing, I repeat, nothing you've said changes that."

The rogue's face changed into a mask of hatred and loathing, his eyes closing to slits as he shouted, spittle flying everywhere as vitriol spewed from him viciously. "I demand the right to a fair fight! I challenge you, Alpha, and if I win I'm taking your goddamn Pack!"

Rafe couldn't help the laugh that tore from him at the pure stupidity of the man. "Really? You're challenging me?"

"Yes! Right here and now."

"You don't have the right to challenge me, you fuckwit. You're a damn prisoner with no rights whatsoever." Rafe shook his head. "But I'll be reasonable and allow you a fight. I can't exactly say a fair fight because you're injured but I don't give a damn about that. Take it or leave it."

"I'll fucking take it!"

Rafe undressed quickly then untied the prisoner, pointing to the door. "After you."

CHAPTER 7

As Rafe followed behind the rogue, Jacy's Wolf nudged his thigh, sending his thoughts through loud and clear.

"I can take care of him for you."

Rafe could feel the pent-up energy inside his Beta. He was raring to go. Jacy wanted to tear into this asshole as much as Rafe did.

"He had my mate in his filthy hands. Threatened her life. No, my friend, this bastard is all mine."

Following the nameless rogue from the cabin, Rafe noticed the sun going down through the trees. The forest sounds reminding him just how precious his land was as small animals hurried around unseen, birds singing their evensong, and the scent of the multitude of plants and wildflowers filled his nostrils. He *had* to protect this.

It had been his family's for generations, many hundreds of years ago they'd settled here in the plush, but wild land. He loved it as much as he loved anything and he'd die before he would allow anyone to destroy his home, his Pack, everyone he loved, including the mate he'd been certain he didn't need.

How foolish had he been?

Tasha meant everything to him and he couldn't wait to return to her and finally hold her to him as his lips found hers in that first, exquisite kiss. First he would deal with the lowlife that had dared to hunt her down and put his soiled hands on her perfection.

"Rafe!"

Jacy's yell in his head brought him out of his inner thoughts with a jolt. The rogue already transformed and leaping toward him, jaws wide, teeth glinting off the waning sun and with one thought: to rip his head off.

Rafe darted to the side, morphing as he went, barely escaping the rogue's attack. Realizing he'd been too wrapped up in his thoughts, Rafe had given the rogue the opportunity to transform and begin healing its wounds. The Wolf attacking him was a seasoned fighter, then again, he would be if he went around murdering innocents.

Its dirty grey fur rippled as it circled around, trying to catch Rafe off-guard. His own beast snarled viciously before launching toward its opponent, meeting mid-air in a clash of fangs and claws. The scent of blood filled the air as both made contact. Rafe suffering a shallow gouge along his flank as they tumbled on the ground.

In the background, he heard wild-life scatter and run, scared by the battle going on and heading for safety. Saddened that this rogue had caused such chaos to his peaceful haven only made his blood boil all the more. His anger rising to heights Rafe didn't know he was capable of as he focused on destroying the Wolf before him.

Everything around him disappeared. Rafe could only see, focus, and deal with the beast hell-bent on killing him. He knew that wouldn't happen. No matter how strong the rogue thought he was, he could never match a strong Alpha and Rafe was well aware he was one of the strongest. His grandfather and father before him were known for their strength and that had been passed onto him, in spades.

He never abused that power, using it only when the situation required it. This was one of those times. Rafe harnessed every ounce of his supremacy as he barreled into his opponent, knocking him flying through the air to land with a dull thud. His Wolf sprang high into the air, pouncing on top of the dazed rogue, opening his huge jaws and sinking his teeth around its vulnerable neck.

Rafe applied pressure, fangs puncturing skin and sinew as blood spurted to cover his fur with its crimson stain. The metallic scent filling his nostrils as he shook his head from side to side, ripping and shredding until he felt the throat tear away in his jaws. Spitting out the filthy remnants, he moved slightly to encompass the side of the rogue's neck, shredding viciously until he felt bone.

His Wolf savagely continued until the sound of bone breaking rang in its ears. The rogue collapsed beneath him as he released his death-grip, his beast's head rearing up to howl its victory for all to hear.

Bloodlust running rampant through his Wolf, Rafe allowed it for a few moments before taking control. His heart beating wildly in his chest as he transformed, head bowed, drenched in his enemy's blood.

He'd had his fair share of fights, both human and beast, but this was the first time he'd reveled in the death of another. He wasn't sure what to think of that fact, but he didn't have the luxury of time to ponder on it. There was far too much to do to ensure the safety of his people, so he shoved it away into the recesses of his mind to revisit at a later date.

Possibly. He might never think of this bastard again, or how good he felt at ending him. Whatever. He'd done what any good Alpha would do: take out the trash and protect his Pack.

"Are you all right?" Jacy asked, keeping his distance and eyeing him warily.

"I'll feel better when we find who's behind this so I can tear his damn head off."

"Okaaaaaaaaaay," Jacy said slowly. "But for now, are you injured?"

"I'm fine," Rafe said, pausing to take note of his body. Aches and pains, nothing major apart from that and a few scratches.

Now all he wanted to do was get back to his mate and check on her. His insides churning as he wondered whether she'd managed to heal her broken ankle. Rafe had experienced more than his fair share of broken bones, knowing they hurt like a bitch, so he hoped Tasha was feeling better. The thought of his mate in pain caused a visceral reaction deep inside him. One that reinforced his vow to do whatever it took to keep her safe and destroy anything that threatened her.

Rafe took a deep breath in, exhaling slowly to calm himself as his friend spoke, breaking his inner musings.

"I'll get rid of the trash," Jacy sneered as Rafe went to the cabin to grab his clothes.

"Thanks." Rafe nodded, throwing his jeans and boots on quickly. He left his top off, carrying it instead of putting it on and covering it with blood.

"If you need me just holler," Jacy said, his eyes still wary as he watched his Alpha. "Maybe you should go for a run or something. You look a little wired, you might scare your mom and Tasha if you go home looking like that."

Rafe ignored that. "I'll see you in the morning. Before dawn, so we can go to Tasha's place and see if Myrtle can come up with anything. If magic is behind this then we'll need her help and possibly her mother's. I know her mom isn't Pack, but she's a good woman and a strong Witch. She'll help if we need her."

"Yeah," Jacy confirmed. "Her mom is high up in the Witch Council now, she got some kind of promotion last month. She'll be the one to ask if we need them on our side."

"Another damn Council." Rafe shook his head at the thought. "But if we need to then we will."

"You can ask Myrtle to get in touch with her mom if needed. That way you don't have to deal with all the BS."

Rafe smirked, liking that solution very much. "Good thinking. We'll see what happens tomorrow and then decide."

"I freaking *hate* all that magical mojo." Jacy shivered dramatically, his face screwing up. "I much prefer facing a threat head on and dealing with it, not having to worry about some spell or other."

"You and me both, my friend. I'll see you tomorrow."

He didn't hear his Beta's reply as he took off, jogging back toward camp, to his future, his mate. His Tasha.

Rafe felt the adrenaline still pumping through him so he sped up, trying to burn it off before he reached home. His thick thighs pumping hard as he flew through the forest, leaping over fallen trees and darting around blackberry bushes. The further he got from where he'd fought he realized he could sense, hear, and also see the critters of the forest again. Soothing his soul, both man and beast, with the familiar sights and sounds.

Once again he knew he couldn't allow anyone, *anything*, to take this from him and his people.

His resolve hardened as his steps slowed to a walk, the last mile or so calming him in ways only his land could. By the time he reached the camp he felt much better, not relaxed entirely, but not ready to bite someone's head off either.

Skirting the outskirts he could smell a tantalizing aroma wafting toward him, causing him to inhale deeply. He'd know his mother's cooking anywhere and by the smell he was certain it was his favorite: deer steak.

Great! He was starving.

Slowing down he sneaked toward the back porch, silently approaching and careful not to use the stair that creaked, he stopped to look through the window. The scene he spied on had his heart soaring. His mom at the stove, chatting to Tasha who was setting the table. He stayed in place, watching the two people who were the most important to him: his mother and his mate.

Didn't appear there was going to be a problem with them getting on. They appeared to be happy in each other's company, chatting away as they went about the kitchen at ease. His Wolf howled inside his head, desperate to claim Tasha as his and seal their mating bond. *"Cool it,"* Rafe admonished.

Tasha had been through a nightmare and he didn't want to scare her off.

The smell of the cooking food pulled him to the door, opening it and slipping inside. Neither woman noticed him for a few moments but then his mother saw him, her eyes widening in shock.

"Son! Oh my, are you okay?"

Rafe looked down at his naked chest, caked with dried blood, shrugging. "I'm fine. The rogue, not so much."

"I'll be right back." His mom darted away.

Tasha slid around the kitchen table, stopping in front of him. He noticed she wasn't limping. Good. She must have healed while he was gone.

"Are you sure you're not hurt? That's an awful lot of blood." Her pale eyes gazed up at him, worry clearly visible.

He stared down. Taking a moment to feast on

her beauty. She'd had a shower, obviously, as her long auburn hair fell in soft waves down her back and no longer was her face smudged with dirt. She was freaking gorgeous.

Rafe leaned down, stopping when his lips almost touched hers. "I'm fine. It's not my blood."

He couldn't resist inhaling slowly, allowing her delicious fragrance to envelop him. Her eyes widened, pupils dilating, his lips tugging up at the sides at her reaction to him. Tasha's head tilted slightly, bringing her lips to his, but only just. Their skin a mere whisper apart, his mind racing with thoughts of how her soft body would feel against his rock hard one.

Rafe reached up, his fingers running through Tasha's hair to tangle at the base of her neck. Her eyes stayed with his as she moved into his touch. He could wait no longer, his mouth covering hers in their first exquisite kiss. She opened to his tongue's prodding, her fingers slowly caressing his abs as he deepened the kiss.

Her touch was magical as she moved upwards to place her palms on his chest. His cock hardening in his jeans so quickly it surprised him. He knew she felt it, her gasp into his mouth and the quick thud of her heart so erotic he barely contained himself.

He almost picked her up to carry her off to his room. The thought of spending hours learning everything he could about his mate so alluring it was practically impossible to resist. He'd scour her body, and discover what would give her the greatest pleasure. His mind so focused on their kiss and her body against his that he almost growled when his mother rejoined them.

"Hmm, sorry to disturb you two, but Rafe, you need to go get cleaned up."

His mother's interruption felt like being doused in a bucket of ice-cold water. Tasha springing back from him, her cheeks blushing scarlet as one of her fingers ran over her luscious lips. A look of wonder in her pale eyes as she stared at him.

"Later," Rafe whispered before spinning away to go shower and dress in clothes not tainted by the stench of the bastard rogue.

Chapter 8

Rafe stood under the shower, allowing the cascading water to cool his ardor. He only managed to damp it down to a gnawing ache. Much better than the ravenous need he'd felt when he left Tasha though.

His hands splayed on the wall as he regained control. "Dumbass." He ground out thinking of the way he'd almost picked her up and carried her to his room. "She'll need time so just cool your jets."

The water continued to flow over him until finally his cock was no longer steel hard and painful. His ears pricked up, his heart thundering in his chest when a sound he dreaded broke through his inner reprimand.

Crying. Someone, no, not *someone*, Tasha. She was sobbing and the sound elicited emotions in him he'd never encountered before. A hand slammed on the wall as his other turned off the shower, grabbing a towel and wrapping it around his waist he flew out of his room.

Honing in on the sound he stopped at the door to the room Tasha had been in earlier. Her crying calling to him in ways he couldn't control. He *had* to go to her. Help her. Do whatever he could to ease her suffering and grief.

Rafe knocked softly on the door before opening it and going in. Tasha lay on the bed, her face pushed into a pillow as she cried. "Tasha, baby, are you okay?"

Dumb question.

Shaking his head at himself he slowly walked over, sitting on the edge of the bed and patting her back. "I'm sorry."

She turned toward him, eyes red and puffy, cheeks stained by her tears. "What for? You've nothing to be sorry for."

Rafe frowned, confused. "I thought I'd upset you earlier. You know, downstairs, when I kissed you."

He watched as her pale eyes widened as she shook her head, her gorgeous hair flying around. "No, it wasn't you that upset me. It's me that's upset me."

"Uhh? I'm puzzled. How can *you* upset yourself?"

Tasha flipped over onto her back, running a hand down her face as she sniffled. "Because I enjoyed that damn kiss so much."

Her face flushed scarlet as she admitted her reaction to his touch. Rafe barely managed to stop his lips tugging up into a grin, instead he reached out to hold one of her hands. "And that's wrong?"

He asked, more baffled than ever.

Tasha's eyes closed, refusing to meet his stare as she nodded. "My insides are all over the place. I've not even had time to grieve for my parents, my loved ones, or my Pack. Yet here I am all hot and bothered whenever you're anywhere near me. I feel ashamed of how I responded to you. Surely I shouldn't . . ."

Rafe couldn't allow her to continue her tirade against herself, tugging on her hand and pulling her up and into his arms. His embrace was tight as he held her to his naked chest. "I don't ever want you feeling bad about yourself. You're amazing. Shoot, you managed to escape and alert us about this threat to Wolves. You got away and stayed ahead of those fucking rogues. You're strong, brave, and the most beautiful person I've ever met."

Tasha buried her head into his shoulder, her arms circling him and holding onto him as if she were drowning. "I feel so sad inside but then you make me feel anything but sad. It's strange and scary."

"We're soul-mates, Tasha." Rafe ran a hand through her long tresses, marveling at how silky it felt. "Nobody can fight against that. Trust me, I've been trying for days."

"Days?" Tasha looked up into his face, her eyes wide.

"Yeah," Rafe confirmed, a half smile tugging at his mouth. "I've been a little crazy for a while. Always in Wolf form and hunting like crazy. I was eating enough in a day that would normally do me for weeks. I wasn't in control and finally my mom told me about . . ."

"Oh my gosh!" Tasha sprang back from him, her hand flying to her chest. "The Hunger. You had the Hunger?"

Rafe was surprised at the shock on her face as

her eyes twinkled with something other than surprise. He wasn't sure but it looked like she was happy. Weird.

"Yes, I had this hunger thing, apparently." He shrugged. "Because as soon as I actually communicated with my beast and mentioned our mate, it was on board and actually seemed relieved. It was then I came looking for you."

Rafe stopped as the full implication of his pissing around for days hit him. Shit. If he'd started looking earlier then maybe he could've helped Tasha's Pack. His heart almost stopped beating, his eyes dropping guiltily from hers.

"Rafe?" Tasha scooted closer, a finger tipping his chin down so she could see him. "You couldn't have done anything. I promise."

He couldn't stop the remorse inside him, eating away at his guts. "Maybe I could have. I'll never know because I was so . . ."

Rafe stopped, unable to continue as the weight of his indecision came crashing down upon him.

Tasha moved closer, her hands either side of his face as she gazed into his eyes. "How long ago did the hunger take over you?"

"Days ago," he admitted sadly.

"I've been on the run for more than a week, in fact it's more like ten days," she whispered. "By the time your hunger struck, my Pack was already doomed. It's not your fault, Rafe."

"Then why do I feel so guilty?" Rafe asked quietly.

"Because you're a good man," she muttered before her lips touched his in a brief kiss. "One that I look forward to getting to know better."

"I promise I'll get to the bottom of this," Rafe told her firmly. "I'll find out who did this to your Pack and . . ."

Tasha's finger on his lips shut him up. "I know you will."

Rafe nodded. "I'm sorry I didn't come for you sooner."

"That's behind us now. I'm just amazed that you went through the hunger." She raised an eyebrow. "I've heard tales about it and some Wolves go nuts. And by nuts I mean completely losing their human side and turning feral. It's quite scary you went through it. I might've lost you too."

"I did think I was losing my mind at times," Rafe admitted, both to Tasha and himself.

He dropped his head back, looking at the

ceiling as he exhaled loudly. That little snippet causing him to realize he'd almost lost everything: his mate and his Pack.

His stomach lurched at the thought. Pack was everything to him and he'd worked damn hard since taking over from his father to ensure they flourished under him. He would do anything for his Wolves but he'd almost allowed it to slip away. That wasn't something he'd forget anytime soon.

"Hey—" Tasha's soft voice brought him back to the present, his eyes dropping to lock with hers. "You made it through. That's a feat all in itself, many don't."

"I nearly lost everything." Rafe couldn't still his rapid heartbeats as he continued to think of what could have happened.

"But you didn't." Tasha reached up, her soft hand caressing his face. "You didn't lose your Pack, or me, or, more importantly, yourself."

"Tasha." Rafe's voice came out low, husky, full of emotion as he leaned into her touch. "I've seen this before, other Wolves when they've met their mate, but damn it, I never understood. Not until I saw you in that fucker's arms in the forest. At that moment I would've taken on Satan himself to free you. I couldn't bear it that he was touching you, threatening you. It almost was my undoing."

"I know." She gave him a shy smile, her eyes coming to life and twinkling up at him. "I felt our pull earlier. I'd jumped over a little stream that cut through the forest and as soon as my feet landed I saw your Wolf in my head. It was bizarre but I had to push it away. I knew they weren't far behind me so I pushed on until I ended up falling down a dang rabbit hole. Just like me to do something stupid like that."

He could feel her, sense how her emotions were warring inside her. She wanted him. There was no doubt about that but he could also feel her holding back. No matter. He'd wait for his Tasha to be ready to take the next step.

Rafe huffed out a breath as images of what that *next step* would be: her luscious body beneath his as he took her, body and soul, to ecstasy.

"What are you thinking?" Tasha asked, her head tilted to the side. Her eyes so damn gorgeous as she gazed up at him through her long dark lashes.

He chuckled. "That's not something I'd like to admit right now."

"Oh." Her eyes widened as her mouth dropped open, a flush creeping up her neck.

She was the most exquisite thing he'd ever seen and he wanted nothing more than to devour her and cause her to scream his name. Rafe tried to rise. "I think I better go before I do something that I shouldn't."

Tasha's hand landed on his thigh, holding him in place. "Can we kiss?"

"Babe," Rafe groaned as blood rushed south to breathe life into his cock. "We can kiss anytime you want. I just don't want to pressure you . . . ya know . . . about the rest of it."

"My Wolf is giving me a headache," Tasha whispered.

"Mine too." Rafe smiled, reaching to entwine his fingers in her hair at the base of her neck. "The mating call is driving me crazy, but I know you need time, sweetheart."

Tasha leaned forward, her lips brushing along his chest. Damn, he should've put clothes on. If she continued doing that he was certain he'd embarrass himself. When her tongue darted out and licked around one of his nipples he hissed through his teeth.

"Damn, Tash, you better stop or . . ."

"Or what?" She looked up, her eyes hooded and her pupils dilated to almost encompass her entire eye, leaving only a slight rim of grey around it.

"I think you know what." Rafe smirked down at her.

"Rafe." Tasha kissed first one nipple then the other before glancing up at him. "Would it be so wrong of me to want this now? To want to mate with you? I know it sounds weird, we barely know each other but . . ."

"You are my mate, Tasha, time won't change that." Rafe raised an eyebrow. "The only thing time will give us is getting to know each other, our likes, dislikes but regardless of all of that, we are mates. I want to mark you as mine but I don't want to force you into anything. Not with everything you've gone through."

"I don't want to be alone," Tasha sighed. "I mean tonight. I don't want to sleep alone. I'm still scared and I feel guilty about wanting to do *stuff* with you but then I think of what my mom would say. I know she'd tell me to 'get my head out of my ass and mate already'."

"Sounds like she was a wise woman," Rafe said solemnly. "I'd much rather you were beside me tonight too, so, I guess tonight we'll sleep in my room. What do you say?"

Rafe knew it would be the most extreme torture to have her in his bed, lying next to him yet not seal their bond. He'd spend half the night under a cold shower.

"I think I'd like that."

He pulled her head toward his, desperate to feel the sweetness of her mouth once again. Tasha moaning into his mouth forcing every last drop of blood in his brain to drop to his groin. Rafe deepened the kiss, her hands running across his bare skin and causing his cock to throb with need to be inside his mate. He clearly heard her heart speed up, keeping pace with his own, as their tongues danced together in a tango of lava hot desire.

He never wanted this moment to end. His mate in his arms, responding to his touch, her desire matching his.

Then he was drenched in ice-cold water when his mom yelled, "Where are you two? Dinner's ready."

Reluctantly pulling back, Tasha's eyes widening as she looked at the tent in his towel. "Sorry, you've gotten me all hot and bothered. I'd better go and try and get rid of this before I go down."

Tasha's head fell back, laughter erupting. Her

hand flew up to stifle it as she gasped. "Yeah, you better. I'm sure that's not something any mom wants to see."

Rafe chuckled along with her. Happy that her earlier sadness seemed to have abated. "I'll be down shortly."

"Don't call me shortly." Tasha grinned cheekily.

"What?" Rafe frowned, taking him a few seconds to get the joke. "Oh, very funny."

"I thought so," Tasha quipped as she rose. "I'll wash up and see you downstairs."

"Definitely." Rafe gripped the towel that showed his arousal. "I might have to slip in for a cold shower first."

Tasha burst out laughing again as she disappeared into the bathroom. He was certain it was the finest sound he'd ever heard. Her merriment following him down the corridor. It was far better than hearing her sobbing, that was for damn sure.

Rafe thought he'd do anything in his power to hear her laughing every damn day. Shit, he'd do whatever he could to make that happen. Any damn thing.

He would be counting the hours, minutes, the

freaking seconds until he held her in his arms, in his bed, and made her his for eternity. It couldn't come quick enough. Maybe he should drop some hints and see if his mother would stay with a friend tonight? No, he'd said he would wait and that's what he'd do, even though he was desperate to make Tasha his he also knew she needed time to mourn.

Chapter 9

Jacy greeted him when he finally made it downstairs. He'd had to spend an uncomfortable five minutes having that cold shower he'd mentioned before he was able to dress.

His best friend eyed him closely as he raised a hand. "Hi, how're you feeling after earlier?"

"I'm fine," Rafe said honestly. He had no trouble in taking out the rogue. None whatsoever. He'd do it again if he had the chance just because the dirty mutt had touched his precious mate.

"Okay, good to know." Jacy smiled over at Tasha. "How're you settling in? Is there anything I can do for you? If so, just ask."

Rafe couldn't stop the rumbled growl that

erupted, his teeth baring as he snapped, "That's not necessary."

Ellie shook her head as she placed a huge pot in the middle of the table. "Rafe, behave yourself. Sit down and everyone tuck in."

"Where's my steak?" Rafe grumbled when he saw the hotpot. "I smelt it earlier, deer, where is it?"

Jacy smirked. "I ate it while we were waiting on you."

Rafe threw a filthy look toward his Beta. "That better be a joke."

"Nope." Jacy held out his hands. "Sorry, but I was hungry and it was just sitting there. I couldn't resist."

Rafe scowled, his eyes slitting to glare at Jacy. His mom smacked his back as she returned from the stove. "He's pulling your leg, Son. Here's your steak. It might be a little dried out because you were away for so long and I had to keep it warm in the oven."

His eyes scooted to Tasha's noting the blush and shy smile as she gazed back. "Sorry, I was filthy. It took me a while to get clean."

Tasha's eyes dropped and he was certain she was trying not to giggle. The sight making him want her all the more. Then he realized where she sat, too far away.

"Tasha,"—he reached over, pulling out the chair right next to him—"Come and sit here."

She cocked an eyebrow but did as he said, sitting down and looking at him questioningly. He shrugged. "You were too far away."

Her eyes sparkled, her smile wide as she nodded. "I think that's one of the nicest things a man's ever said to me."

"Really?" Jacy butt in. "Then you've been seeing the wrong men, gorgeous."

Rafe slammed his hands down on the table, silverware clattering around as he snarled across the table. Anger rising quickly inside him as he raged at his Beta. "If you don't shut your mouth I'll do it for you."

Tasha reached over, her hand grasping one of his hands and squeezing it. "He's only joking, Rafe."

"I don't care," Rafe ground out. "This is my *mate*. Do you understand? She is therefore your Alpha too. Show some respect."

Jacy lowered his head for a brief moment before peeking up. "I apologize. I meant no disrespect."

"You didn't do anything wrong." Ellie patted

Jacy on the shoulder as she passed by, her withering stare making Rafe feel like an errant toddler. "Rafe, you and Tasha have to mate. The sooner the better, before you rip someone's head off for daring to even glance in her direction. Jacy, as you damn well know, jokes . . . a lot. He didn't mean anything by it."

Glancing at Tasha he noticed her blush, the scarlet tinge glowing on her beautiful face as she inclined her head and waggled her eyebrows. He got the message, loud and clear.

"Mom," Rafe started in a gruff voice. "Do you think you could . . ."

"Don't even say it." She shook her finger at him. "I'm waaaaay ahead of you, Son. I'm going to stay with Myrtle tonight so you two have the place to yourselves. In fact, I plan on sleeping there for some time."

Rafe grinned then felt a hard pinch at his side, turning to see Tasha frowning and giving a quick nod toward Jacy. He frowned but she pinched him again so he relented, coughing to clear his throat first. "Jacy, sorry about that."

"That's okay," Jacy said solemnly. "I didn't mean to upset either of you and I know how strung out you've been, Rafe. I should know when to hold my tongue."

"Nah." Rafe shook his head. "It's my fault. I just have a lot on my mind."

"Have you called the dreaded Council yet?" Jacy asked in a mock-horror-film voice.

"I'll do it after I've eaten," Rafe replied slowly. "I've been putting it off. You know what Atherton blinking Denholm is like, he's a pain in the ass, but we need them on this. So I'll put up with his moaning and talking to me as if I were a five year old."

Ellie laughed. "You act like one often enough."

Tasha stifled a giggle as Jacy chuckled, in full agreement with his mom but being smart enough not to voice his thoughts.

"Can we eat?" Rafe said instead.

Jacy nodded enthusiastically. "At last! I'm starving."

"You boys, there's no keeping up with you." Ellie shook her head, smiling indulgently.

The next hour passed quickly, Tasha at ease with his family. Jacy might not be blood but he was definitely Rafe's brother so it meant a lot that they got on. They would be working together running the Pack once the threat had been dealt with and they could get back to some semblance of normality. His mom and Tasha seemed to hit it off well and that was another relief for him. She was all he had left since they'd lost his father, he would hate it if they didn't get along. Didn't look like that would be a problem though as he rose to leave them chattering at the table.

"I'll be back as soon as I've spoken to the Council. Jacy, stay put in case I need to discuss anything with you."

"Sure," Jacy answered as he shoveled another piece of his mom's lemon pie into his mouth.

Rafe wasn't looking forward to the call but he'd get it over and done with, and then at least he'd have a better idea of what their next steps would be.

Closing the office door he took a moment to look around, not quite feeling at home here yet. He still missed his dad and every time he came in here the loss hit him like a shovel to the face. After all, this had been his father's domain and those were a huge pair of shoes to fill. He'd done his best since they'd lost him, even opening up a couple more businesses in the nearby town. One of which was a huge success.

Who woulda thought that a Shifter bar would go down so well in middle-America? Especially when most humans were shit-scared of anything supernatural, Wolves included. More than a few obviously liked to live "on the wild side" so to speak.

It had though and brought in much needed funds for the Pack, as well as employing almost two dozen. He thought his father would've been aghast at the idea but that didn't stop Rafe. He'd do whatever it took to ensure the continued prosperity for his people. Anything at all.

"Get it over with," he said aloud, knowing he was procrastinating. He sat on the corner of the huge antique wooden desk, picked up the phone and made the call.

"Are you all right?" Tasha jumped up as he returned to the kitchen. "You've been away for ages."

Rafe checked the clock on the wall above the window. Over a damn hour that old fart Atherton had kept him on the line, going over and over everything. He'd barely managed to stop himself from cursing and hanging up.

"I'm fine." Rafe reached out, cupping her face and rubbing his thumb over her lips. "Atherton made me tell him everything ten times over and even then he wanted to hear it all again."

"Oh dear." Tasha leaned into his touch as she spoke.

"So what's happening?" Jacy asked and Rafe noticed that his mother was nowhere in sight. He guessed she must've gone to Myrtle's already.

"He'll be sending a team out to the Pack to deal with burying them and he's also going to send his top Enforcer to help us."

Rafe paused, waiting, and it was a mere second before Jacy whistled. "Do you mean Zohar? The almighty and powerful Zohar Drake is coming here?"

The sarcasm hung in the room as Rafe nodded. "Yes, he certainly is."

"Fuck," Jacy spat out. "Oh, sorry, Tasha but that guy is . . ."

"Intense is the word you're looking for, buddy." Rafe chuckled. "Wanna beer?"

"Hell yes." Jacy nodded vigorously. "We'll all need to be on top of our game with Zohar around."

"Who's Zohar?" Tasha asked as she went to the massive double door fridge, opened it and grabbed some beers.

"You didn't need to do that, I would've gotten them." Rafe told her as he sat back down at the head of the table, tossing a beer to Jacy and opening one for himself.

"No worries," she smiled. "I'm used to getting . . ." she paused, her voice lowering to barely a whisper. "I mean I was used to getting them for my dad."

"Sorry," Rafe said up at her, reaching for her arm and pulling her onto his lap where he engulfed her within his embrace. Kissing the top of her head as she took several deep breaths.

"No, it's all right," she said quietly. "I sometimes forget, ya know?"

"Yes," Rafe said somberly. "I remember doing the same when my dad died. It gets better, I promise."

"Thanks." She smiled sadly up at him. "Now tell me, who is this guy you're talking about?"

Jacy snickered as Rafe inhaled, exhaled then started. "Zohar Drake is the Council's top Enforcer. He deals with their worst cases and he's rather . . . *intense*."

"That's one word for what he is," Jacy sneered. "Downright cold, hard and *cold.* He's a fucking machine. Pardon my French."

"Don't apologize." Tasha shot Jacy a quick grin. "I can cuss along with the best so no need to worry on my account."

"Anyway," Rafe carried on. "Zohar will be meeting us tomorrow and then he'll be living here until this has been dealt with."

"Oh goody." Jacy clapped his hands, his tone as sarcastic as Rafe had ever heard.

"I know, but he is the best and he has some unique abilities that we don't have."

"Like what?" Tasha asked.

"He can transform quicker than anything I've ever seen," Rafe shook his head. "Damnedest thing to watch but I've seen it. That can come in handy at times, especially as his beast is huge."

"Bigger than yours?" Tasha asked, wide-eyed.

"Yes," Rafe said, hating to admit it.

"Damn, he must be a freak," Tasha said seriously.

Jacy chuckled. "I agree with you there, sister."

Rafe noted how at ease she was in Jacy's company. It actually made him happy now, his jealousy abating with their impending mating. It meant she wouldn't be scared if he had to leave her in his Beta's care.

"Anyway," he carried on. "The Council is as shocked as we are at what's happened and they're sending out a ton of other Enforcers, some with magical abilities, to search the area. They're hoping that we can find who is behind this and stop him from repeating this grotesque extermination of a Pack from happening again."

Jacy's face was grim as he nodded, Tasha's was a mixture of sadness, grief, and anger.

Rafe understood. As Alpha, his feelings were a combination of all those too but at this moment anger was taking the lead. He couldn't wait to dole out some justice for the Pack that had been destroyed.

Chapter 10

After they'd finished discussing what Atherton Denholm had said, Jacy slid out of his chair, stretching. "I'm going to get some rest. Tomorrow is going to be a long day."

"See you out front just before dawn," Rafe reminded him.

"Yeah, I'll be there."

Jacy disappeared out the back door as Rafe turned to Tasha. She looked nervous and worried, nibbling her bottom lip and picking at the skin on one of her fingers. So much so that she drew blood. What the hell?

"Tasha, are you okay?" Rafe asked quietly.

Her eyes remained downcast, refusing to meet

his. "Tash?"

Finally she raised hers and the conflict he saw staring back clenched his stomach tight. "What's wrong?"

"Promise you won't be mad at me?" she pleaded softly.

"I won't be mad," he assured her.

"Can we wait? You know . . . to seal our mating?" She looked so upset that her words took a moment to sink in.

Dang! Struggling to mask his disappointment and hoping he'd managed, he said, "Of course, baby, if that's what you want."

"I'm sorry," she sobbed, her voice hitching as she fought to stop her tears from falling.

"Don't." He reached over, wiping a stray tear from her soft cheek.

"I know you said no earlier and I don't want to argue, but . . ."

He held up a hand. "Oh shit, any sentence that starts that way usually ends up in an argument."

"I'm going with you tomorrow."

Her voice was firm, her eyes locked with Rafe's as she waited on a reply. Fuck! The last thing on this earth he wanted was her being there tomorrow. Shoot, he couldn't even imagine how it would affect her seeing her Pack like that.

Dead. Every last one of them murdered. It was the thing of damn nightmares and *not* something he wanted to subject his mate to.

"If you refuse I'll go anyway, on my own." Her chin jutted out defiantly but to Rafe she looked adorable.

"Rebellious much?" he asked, head tilting to the side as he stared hard at her.

Anyone in the Pack would have backed down, without a second's thought. Not Tasha.

Her head lifted as she nodded. "My mom used to say that all the time. I don't like just being told what to do. Not if I have an opinion on something. And on *this*, I definitely have my own opinion. I have to go, Rafe. I don't have a choice."

"Sure you do," he answered, using his firm Alpha voice. "You can do as I ask and stay here, where you'll be safe."

"I'm not sure if you understand," she implored. "First, it's my Pack! I have to go. Second, I feel safer the nearer I am to you. I won't stay here alone."

Rafe couldn't help the exasperated sigh that exploded from him as he pushed his chair back and started pacing. "Tasha, you wouldn't be alone. You'd be here with my Pack and a dozen guards with one order: to keep you safe. I have no idea what we'll be walking into tomorrow. What if there are rogues still there and they attack? I need to be able to fight without worrying about you being hurt, or worse. I almost lost you before. I couldn't stand losing you, my mate. I just couldn't."

"Yet you expect me to sit here and wait for you?" she said hotly, her face flushed with anger. "While you go off and possibly face rogues? That is *not* happening, Rafe. Not in a million years. I am . . ."

He strode over quickly, grabbed her shoulders and lifted her up, cutting off her tirade. "You're my mate and the thought of you being hurt is like a knife in my fucking guts."

"Ditto!" she snarled back. The fire in her eyes bringing out sparks of silver in the pale grey that he hadn't noticed before. Her clenched fists on his chest between them as her anger grew.

"Touché." Rafe leaned down, his forehead on hers as he tried to control his breathing. "Okay, if I say you can come, will you promise to follow my orders? That's what every other Wolf will be doing,

Tasha. I *am* Alpha."

He watched as her anger dimmed but her fire did not. He liked that. He needed a mate that was strong and could stand up to him when required. Even if that would piss him off.

Her nod was so faint that he almost missed it. Her voice reluctant as she agreed. "Fine."

"Thank you," he sighed as relief flooded through him. "You are too precious to me, Tasha. I can't allow anything to happen to you, sweetheart."

"I know," she said, relaxing against his chest.

"I have to text Jacy to rearrange things for tomorrow." He snatched his phone from his pocket, moving away. "If you're coming with us then I'm taking the extra guards too."

"I'm definitely coming," she said firmly.

"I can't change your mind?" He tried one last time.

"Nope," she said, shaking her head.

Finishing his text, he returned, his finger running down her cheek. "You're going to keep me on my toes. Aren't you?"

She smirked, shrugging. "Probably."

"You need to listen to me tomorrow, stay close by and if I tell you to do something, baby, please don't argue."

"I'll try my very best." She made a cross over her heart before yawning. "I'm tired, can we go to bed?"

Rafe's heart sped up. Could he have her close but not mate with her?

He'd have to. He refused to hurt her in any way and if she needed to wait for a day or so then he'd just have to man up. He would have to ask her something though. He'd wait until they were settled in his room first.

"Let's go up," he said instead, taking her hand and leading her upstairs.

"Rafe, in case you're wondering, I don't want to sleep alone. I just don't want us to . . . you know. Not until I've buried my parents. It seems wrong somehow."

Her emotion-filled words tore at his heart. He wished he could take her pain away but he knew he couldn't. What he could do was respect her wishes and be there for her. No matter what.

"I understand and it's all right." He smiled down at her. "I'll wait for you, baby."

"Thank you," she said softly as they walked along the hallway to his room.

Opening the door, he waved an arm around, showing her the room that would now be theirs. It was manly, nothing in it feminine at all, and he expected that to change. He was fine with that too. He didn't care what his surroundings were. Only that each night his mate lay beside him. *That* was the most important thing of all.

"I know you'll want to change it and that's all right. I don't give a hoot about any of that. All I care about is that we're together."

His voice had dropped, his feelings overcoming him as Tasha walked around. She looked over and gave him a smile that would be imprinted forever on his brain. Her eyes twinkling with mischief.

"You might regret saying that," she quipped. "What if I want pink walls and ruffles everywhere?"

Rafe winced. Pink walls? Shit, he hoped not.

"Emm, that's fine with me," he replied bravely.

Tasha spun around, her arms wide, singing. "Liar, liar, pants on fire."

Laughter filled the room as he cracked up, unable to hold it in. Tasha stopped spinning, giggling along with him until tears ran down her cheeks and she held her sides. She flopped onto the bed where her laughter finally died down.

"I'm not a 'frilly' type of gal, so you've no worries on that score."

"Thank fu . . ." He stopped. "Sorry, you know what I mean though."

"Will you stop that?" Tasha sat up, frowning. "You can cuss if you want. It doesn't offend me. Let's be honest . . . sometimes fuck is the only word that works . . . right?"

He couldn't help but laugh, chuckling as he nodded in agreement. "Yeah."

She got off the bed, looking around and looking embarrassed. "I don't have much with me. I just grabbed a few things when I ran so I don't even have anything to wear to bed."

"No problem." He walked into his huge wardrobe, fumbling around in a drawer and coming out with one of his t-shirts. "This should do you for now, until we can get your things from home. There's also spare toothbrushes in the bathroom cabinet. Help yourself to anything you need."

"Thanks." She took the substitute nightwear and headed into the bathroom, closing the door.

Running a hand through his hair, Rafe knew he'd have to talk to her when she returned. He *had* to. There was no dodging what he needed to say. He only hoped she didn't freak out and refuse. That would not be good for him, or his beast. His Wolf had been prowling around in his head since they'd first found her. Its desperation to make her their mate was all-consuming and he was finding it difficult to control it. He hoped the compromise he'd come up with would settle it down, for now.

That would only work if Tasha agreed though.

He undressed then went in search of a pair of pajama bottoms. He doubted he'd find any. It wasn't as if he wore anything to bed but he didn't think Tasha would be too happy if he jumped in au-naturale so he snagged an old pair of sweat pants and used those instead.

They were worn and loose, hanging low down on his hips, but they were better than nothing.

As he walked out of the walk-in closet, Tasha exited the bathroom. His breath caught in his throat, she looked adorable in his tee which hung to her mid-thigh, but she also looked scared and vulnerable. His inner-Alpha sprang forth forcing him to stride over and take her into his arms to comfort her.

He rubbed a hand up and down her back, his other grasping her head to his chest. Her hands splayed on his bare chest as he whispered, "It'll get better, sweetheart. I promise it will. It'll take time, but I'll always be here for you. Anything you need, anytime, just ask."

"I guess it's just hitting me properly now," she gasped, her breath whispering against his skin. "Before, all I thought about was keeping ahead of the rogues chasing me. Now all I can think about is that everyone I've ever loved and cared about are gone. Not one of them is left alive, Rafe, not one."

"I know." He used his power, sending calmness and serenity toward her. "Once we've had a funeral, you will be able to take the next step in the grieving process and I'll be right there with you. You won't take that journey alone, my love."

Continuing to hold her, his power washing over her, he finally felt her body relax against his. His Wolf pranced about, pawing at the ground and howling. "I know you're tired but before we go to sleep, I need to ask you something."

Her head tilted back, her sorrow-filled eyes searching his. "What?"

"I respect your decision not to mate right now." He leaned down so their eyes were level. "But my Wolf is going to drive me insane, so would you allow me to mark you? I promise I won't take it further than that. I just *need* to know that everyone is aware that you are mine. Not just for my own damn sanity, but it also bestows my Alpha protection to you. That in itself will calm my Wolf down a little and certainly make me feel better. You will be Alpha marked and only a fool would try and hurt you."

He waited, breathless, on her response.

Her eyes widened, little sparkles appearing as they crinkled at the sides and she gave him a smile. "You could do that? I mean . . . mark me without . . . you know?"

His body ached for hers. Physically craved his mate like nothing he'd ever felt before, so much so it hurt. His skin yearned for her touch, his fingers burned with desire to explore every damn inch of her body, his cock throbbed with the need to be inside her. But he would not push his own selfish desires onto his grieving mate.

He was Alpha and he would never do such a thing, so he hugged her a little tighter and nodded. "I'll do whatever it takes, Tasha. I said I'd wait and I will. However, if I don't mark you, I think my beast might just drive me insane enough to have me committed to a loony bin."

"We can't have that now, can we?" she said seriously. "I need you to know something too."

She stopped, nibbling her bottom lip as a blush crept up her neck to cover her cheeks. Rafe almost groaned at the sight. He was desperate to plunder her lips but held himself in check. "What?" he asked instead.

"It's not that I don't want to . . . ya know." Her face grew even redder. "Because I do. You make me feel . . . I guess the way I make you feel. But I just can't. Not with my mom and dad just lying there. It seems so wrong. I need to put them to rest before I can carry on."

"I totally understand that and I'm not pushing you to mate with me tonight," he reiterated. "I just need to settle down my beast and my soul. Knowing you have my mark will do both."

Tasha leaned away, her head tilted to the side, giving a clear view of her neck. Soft skin called to him, pulling him toward it but he stopped short, keeping a firm grip on himself as he asked, "Is that a yes?"

She licked her lips causing his heart to thunder in his chest before she replied, "Yes."

Rafe's beast howled with glee, leaping high

into the air with joy as he took a deep breath to steady himself. "Thank you. It's an honor, Tasha. One I take great responsibility for."

Her eyes fluttered closed as he leaned down, his tongue licking along her skin, sending shudders through her. His arms tightened around her, holding her close so he could feel every single sensation as it affected her. Her breathing increased, little pants as his mouth latched onto the sensitive spot between neck and shoulder, kissing and suckling to ease the tension he now felt in her.

One hand reached up to hold the back of her head, keeping it angled so he had full access, while the other wrapped all the way around her. His fingers barely skimming the side of her breast as he allowed his fangs to descend. This is the moment he'd been dreaming off: claiming his mate.

Even if they would not consummate their joining tonight.

He felt her hand in his hair, her fingers tangling and holding on tightly. Her other trapped between their bodies, resting on his bare skin right above his low-slung sweats. Damn! What he would do for her hand to dip down lower. His cock now straining between them, she must feel it. The steel length rubbed against her belly as he opened his mouth and bit down, hard.

As his fangs broke her skin, she shuddered in his arms, her fingers digging into his scalp as he hungrily gulped her blood down. The sweet taste like nectar as it coated his tongue and throat. Rafe knew nothing would ever be the same in his life again. No. Not when he felt the first strings of their mating taking hold and binding them together.

Holy freaking hell. It was like nothing he'd ever thought possible. His entire being focused on Tasha, her body, her scent, her everything. Their bond swept through him, taking hold deep in his soul, the sensation overwhelming and in a strange way, peaceful. His cock throbbed with need but he forced all thought of consummation from his mind. He'd respect her wishes and would bide his time. When he and Tasha first joined together fully, he wanted it to be a mind-shattering joyous occasion, not overshadowed with her parents' death.

Releasing her neck he quickly slashed his wrist, offering it to her. "This will help seal us together, my mate."

Her eyes were glassy, hooded, and a little confused as she stuck her tongue out, lapping at his blood. It took mere moments for their bond to increase. He felt it, and he could tell she did too. Her eyes spun to lock with his in wonder. Her mouth popped open in a silent "oh" before he covered it with his.

Rafe kept their kiss short, knowing if he didn't that he would be loathe to stop. Tasha's little moan of annoyance when he pulled away had him smiling cockily down at her. "Powerful stuff this mating thing, isn't it?"

She looked dazed as she nodded, murmuring. "Yes. If I knew how powerful it was I think I would've asked to sit down. My legs are like jello."

"No problem." He smirked, picking her up swiftly and carrying her to the bed. "Now you need to get some rest. We have a long day ahead of us tomorrow, sweetheart."

When she didn't respond, he looked down, she was already asleep. Rafe covered her with the comforter before sliding in next to her, pulling his mate next to him and holding her close. Now she was his and he'd never let her go.

Never, and god help anyone who tried to take her from him. He'd tear them limb from limb for even thinking about it.

CHAPTER 11

Tasha's soft moan caused Rafe to glance over, her face white and drawn as they drew nearer to her Pack. Her fist at her mouth as if she were trying not to scream.

He guessed that to be the case and he couldn't blame her. They were about to enter a graveyard. One where they'd find her parents slaughtered in their home. Fuck. He wasn't sure he'd be able to hold his shit together if he were in her shoes.

"I'm right here with you." Reaching over, he snatched her hand, grabbing it tightly. "If you want to leave, just give me the word and I'll have Levi and some guards escort you home."

Her eyes spun to his, her voice strangled as she ground out, "This *was* my home."

"Sorry," he said, mentally kicking himself.

"You know what I meant and . . ."

"Watch out!"

Tasha's squeal had his eyes back on the dirt road, swerving to barely miss hitting a large man standing, arms crossed. "Fucking idiot."

Slamming on the brakes Rafe jumped out, shouting. "What the fuck? You got a death wish?"

The man came over, inscrutable eyes meeting the Alpha's. "I've been waiting on you. We've been here for hours."

Tasha grabbed Rafe's arm. "Who is he and what's going on?"

The rest of their convoy had skidded to a halt, Jacy, Levi and several guards joining them. Rafe patted Tasha's hand. "It's all right, Tasha. This is Zohar, he's from the Council."

The Council Enforcer looked around then nodded toward the Camp that was now visible. "My men have already started working. There are teams digging a large grave in the field behind the camp. Also, there are others dealing with the dead. They are preparing them for burial and taking note of names and other pertinent data to be logged with the Council. Anything which could help us is being passed to me directly."

Tasha stepped forward, her voice wobbling as she tried to make eye contact with the intimidating Enforcer. "Excuse me."

Zohar ignored her, talking over her directly to Rafe. "I'd like your men to . . ."

Rafe snarled, loudly, stepping forward to stand toe to toe with a startled Zohar. "Do not ignore my mate. If you do then we are going to have a huge fucking problem."

"What?" Zohar looked down, he was taller than Rafe and Tasha barely came to his chest. "Who is this?"

"This is Tasha and she is not only my mate but she also escaped from this slaughter." Rafe prodded Zohar's chest. "So she is the *only* fucking witness you have. Listen up, asshole, because she's the only person you can ask about what went down here."

Tasha gasped as Rafe stepped back, his arm going around her waist and drawing her close to his side. Her eyes rose to meet his, her thanks in the look that passed between them.

Zohar huffed. "Whatever. So, what were you going to say?"

"I was about to say that my parents are in there,"—she pointed to the camp—"and I want to see where they are taken for burial. I want to lay them to rest, please. After that, I'll answer any of your questions but first I need to say goodbye to my mom and dad."

Rafe watched her intently as she spoke, heard the slight waver in her voice as she finished. Her chin jutting out as if daring Zohar to disagree only making him love her all the more. His chest puffing out as his arm tightened around her, letting her know he was right there with her.

His eyes switched to the Enforcer. Zohar's jaw clenched and his left eye twitched. A sure sign he was annoyed. Rafe waited, ready to pounce if the man upset Tasha in any way.

Zohar looked off to the side for a moment then back down at Tasha, giving a slight nod. "Fine, go ahead but you'll have to be quick. My men are moving fast to get the job done and I've no idea if they've already dealt with your home or not."

Tasha looked up at Rafe who motioned to Levi. "Levi, get a couple of men and go with her. Don't let her out of your sight."

"On it, boss." Levi pointed to two of his guards who jogged over.

"Thank you," Tasha said to both Zohar and

Rafe.

"I'll catch up with you later," Rafe said quietly, leaning down to kiss her quickly before she left.

"So you've found a mate?" Zohar said with a sneer. "Next you'll have a dozen pups running around your heels."

Zohar's tone more than his words set Rafe's nerves on edge, his anger rising, and his blood on a slow boil. As always. He cracked his neck, side to side, exhaling before he met the Enforcer's eyes. "Shut the fuck up unless it's to do with what's happened here. My life, my mate, it's off limits to you. Understand?"

The Enforcer smirked, as if annoying Rafe was all he'd wanted. Damn it. Rafe knew it. It was how Zohar worked but every damn time he allowed the man to get under his skin. They'd come to blows more than once and if he continued to make remarks about Tasha then they'd do so again, and they did *not* have time for that shit right now.

"We have to find who is behind this so cut the crap." Rafe snarled viciously, allowing his full Alpha power free rein.

He heard several of his men step forward, ready to fight for him, but he held up a hand halting them. This only seemed to amuse Zohar all the more.

"There is magic in the air," Zohar announced in a matter of fact voice, as if the last minute or two hadn't happened.

What the fuck was wrong with this guy? Rafe had no clue. He only knew the Enforcer liked to rub people up the wrong way then sit back and watch the fall out. Asshole.

"Myrtle," Rafe called out, looking for the Healer. She appeared from behind his men, obviously nervous and unwilling to come forward. "It's all right. This asswipe won't harm you."

Myrtle walked slowly toward them, her eyes firmly on Rafe. When she stopped, she refused to look at Zohar, Rafe reached out and patted her shoulder. He could feel her apprehension and hated feeling one of his Pack suffer. "It's all right."

Her eyes sought his, her hands wringing as she nodded. "Magic is here all right. It's stifling and just wrong. It's evil and malevolent. Whoever is using it has bastardized theirs to use it for their own ends. They are powerful and it's possible to track it but I wouldn't, not on our own."

"We can handle whoever is behind this," Zohar scoffed. "Follow me."

Zohar stomped away toward the camp, Rafe shrugged. "Jacy, Myrtle, come with me. The rest of you bring the vehicles."

"Alpha," Myrtle quick-stepped to keep up. "I don't like him. His aura is all . . . wrong. Just wrong."

"It's not his aura I care about. It's whether he can get the job done," Rafe replied grimly.

"He's an ass, don't let him get to you." Jacy tried to help Myrtle who was obviously struggling. "Zohar is the Council's best Enforcer but to hold that position means he has to be a specific type of person. He's not Pack but he usually gets the mission accomplished."

"I still don't like him," Myrtle whined.

"Neither do I," Jacy chimed in as they entered the camp.

Rafe pulled up short, the stench overpowering, cloying in the air, enough to make him gag. Refusing to show any weakness, he opened his mouth, taking shallow breaths through gritted teeth. Jacy cursed as Myrtle let out a sob.

"Oh hell, this is, shoot, I'm gonna throw up."

She ran off, disappearing behind a nearby tree, the sound of her retching almost Rafe's undoing. His jaw aching as he clenched his teeth further, determined not to disgrace himself. "Jacy, check on her then come find me."

"Check on her? Shit, I'll be joining her."

Rafe strode away in search of Tasha, following her scent as clearly as if she'd left him a trail of cookies to follow. Her aroma was sweet and spicy, with a touch of flowery undertones. It drew him forward like a torpedo as he zeroed in on her location. Ignoring everyone around him, brushing aside Zohar as he attempted to talk.

His only thought once he'd entered the camp, the reek of the dead invading his body and soul, was to reach his mate and offer her solace. Her soft cries triggering something deep inside him as he rushed toward her. She stood at the door to a cabin, her home, as Zohar's men carried out two bodies wrapped in white sheets: her parents.

Tears ran down her cheeks, dripping to soak the ground at her feet as she tried to stifle her sobs, a linen hankie stuffed into her mouth. Rafe encompassed her in a warm embrace, full of love and comfort, whispering into her soft tresses. "I'm here, sweetheart. I'll always be here. Lean on me and I'll carry you. I'll take the weight of your grief, you just need to let me."

She leaned back into his body, trembling and shaking. "How?"

Releasing his Alpha power through their virgin mating bond he showed her the way. She gasped as the might of his force touched her, then her body settled, her grief passing to Rafe for him to bear for his mate. It was a heavy load to carry but one he did willingly, Tasha turning into his chest, grabbing him tightly before relaxing.

"I . . . I thought I was going to faint or something. It was so bad, Rafe." She tilted her head, looking up with red-rimmed eyes. "I knew they were dead, I've known since I left. But, seeing them like that, after lying for so many days it was much worse than anything I could've imagined."

"I know, sweetheart, I know." Rafe held her close, rubbing a hand in circles on her back. "Let me help you through this."

"I have no words to thank you," she stuttered before laying her head against his chest.

"You never need to thank me for helping you. You are my mate. I'd die for you, Tasha."

"I'm just realizing that," she gasped.

He wanted to say more, much more, but they were interrupted by Zohar's men leaving. "Miss, if you could follow us now, please."

"What?" She pulled away, dazed. "Oh yes, of course."

Rafe kept an arm around her waist as they walked behind the impromptu pall bearers, following them out of the camp to the mass grave. The stench here was far worse, the sight nothing like Rafe had ever seen and one he prayed he'd never see again.

A massive trench had been dug in the field and it was packed with white wrapped bodies. Line after line, two and three deep, the bodies of the Pack were placed inside their final resting place. Tasha sobbed as her parents joined the rest of the Pack. The men who'd carried them apologizing as they climbed out of the deep hole in the earth.

"Sorry, miss, it was the only way to deal with this amount of bodies."

"I understand," she replied with a voice devoid of emotion.

"If you want, we can take them back to Darkmoon and bury them there?" Rafe told her quietly, her raw despair cloying in his throat.

She took a moment to answer, a brief shake of her head before she said firmly, "No. They should be here, with the rest of the Pack. It's where they belong."

"If you're sure."

"Yes."

Somberly they waited until the last of the bodies were laid to rest, Rafe cradling his mate to his side as she fought to control her tears. He whispered, "It's okay to cry, baby."

But she resolutely shook her head, her body shaking as she raised her chin defiantly. "I'm fine."

He knew better. She was far from fine. The soft sheen of perspiration covering her skin, the thud of her heart, and the unshed tears told him as much, but his mate refused to surrender to her grief.

Myrtle followed behind the men carrying the final dead. Her head bowed reverently as she whispered a farewell. She stopped at the edge of the communal grave, dipping into a purple velvet pouch tied at her waist. Her voice rose as she spoke in a soft but firm tone, honoring the fallen Wolves and sending them on their way to the Goddess.

Then she sprinkled some sort of herbs out onto the bodies. Rafe could taste the scent in the air but didn't try to decipher what was in the concoction as Myrtle lifted her arms high above her and pleaded with the Goddess to take her children home and keep them safe.

Tasha trembled beside him as Myrtle spoke, her body shaking as she choked out, "I love you. Goodbye, Mom, bye, Dad. I promise we'll find who did this and make them pay."

Myrtle came over, grasping one of Tasha's hands, her short curly hair blowing in the wind as she looked up into Tasha's eyes. "I'm so sorry for your loss. If I can help in any way, please, just let me know."

Tasha waited for a moment. Obviously gaining control before she nodded, her voice firm as she replied firmly, "Help us catch who did this. That's all I need right now."

Myrtle's blue eyes seemed all knowing as she tilted her head, studying Tasha. "Revenge doesn't heal all wounds but I'll do whatever I can to help."

"Thank you," Tasha replied, her voice shaking at the end.

Rafe studied his mate, taking in her wide eyes, blood-shot and filled with sorrow. Her body coiled tightly and her breathing coming quickly in short gasps. Her soft full lips pinched together, her cheeks pale with tear tracks visible down the middle. He worried about her and wished she wasn't here to witness this abominable carnage, but he also knew she wouldn't return home, not until they'd dealt with the threat that was still out there.

As the sun shone brightly above, breaking through the few clouds that meandered across the sky, the beams fell directly on the grave. At least some of the bodies were now hidden from view as Zohar's men filled in the trench. More than thirty were working quickly to throw the dirt on top of the Pack. The reek of decomposing bodies abating somewhat as layers of earth gathered over the murdered Pack.

Small mercies in a harrowing situation. Once which Rafe swore would never happen again. He'd make certain of that.

"Myrtle." Rafe broke the silence. "Can you track the magic that's been used here?"

He watched as her face paled, her hands clasping tightly and a small tic appeared at the side of her left eye. She seemed reluctant to answer so he raised an eyebrow, glaring at her. "Well?"

She still faltered, looking down at the ground before she mumbled. "Yes, I could but I wouldn't recommend it. Not until we have someone far more powerful than me in your arsenal. I'm no match for this person, Alpha. If we go after them now then everyone would be in danger."

CHAPTER 12

Rafe wanted nothing more than to hunt down the scumbag responsible for the massacre of this Pack but he wasn't stupid. He wouldn't rush off half-cocked and put any of his Wolves at risk.

The sun beat down on the now covered bodies, newly turned earth mocking him as his body thrummed with anger. Soft hands caressed his chest, looking down into his mate's upturned face full of worry.

"We'll get him . . . them, whoever. But I don't want anyone else to die, Rafe."

Her pale grey eyes implored him, her luscious lips a distraction as he nodded. "I'll figure something out."

"No need." Zohar's deep baritone butted in.

The Enforcer looked between them, his dark

eyes settling on Rafe. "I have someone who can help and they're far more powerful than your half-Witch here."

Myrtle bristled at the insult, her cheeks burning red as Rafe stepped forward, eye to eye with the insolent Zohar. "Don't insult anyone in my Pack. You're in no position to do so, after all, no Pack would have you. Would they?"

Myrtle let out a gasp, Tasha gripped the back of his shirt, but Rafe stood his ground, watching Zohar. His eyes closed to slits, his jaw clenching as he tried to stare down Rafe. Too bad the Enforcer didn't scare him. He'd had more than one run-in with Zohar and no doubt he'd have others, but one thing was for sure: he'd never back down.

A soft breeze ruffled Zohar's dark hair as Rafe glared angrily at him. If anyone else insulted Myrtle he wouldn't have given them a warning, he would've put them in their place right away. It was only because of his position within the Council that he afforded Zohar the luxury of a warning.

Several long moments passed before the Enforcer huffed out a sigh. "Touchy, touchy, Alpha. I thought having a mate was supposed to calm you down."

Rafe's anger mounted, a growl rumbling in his chest, his muscles clenching in readiness for a fight. If this asshole wanted to fight, then today Rafe would give him what he wanted.

"That's enough!" Tasha yelled. "I've just buried my parents and my *entire* Pack! And you two are having a fucking pissing contest. Stop it. Now. Then maybe we can find who is responsible and you can take out all that pent-up rage out on them."

Spinning toward her outraged face, his heart swelled at the sight. She looked fierce. Hands on hips, hair blowing in the wind, eyes wide and angry, face flushed, and damn it, she even had a foot tapping. She was one angry woman and one not to be messed with. Go Tasha.

"I'm sorry." Rafe shrugged. "You're right. We should be focusing on why we're here and nothing else."

Zohar surprised him, stepping forward and giving a small bow. What the hell was that?

He then stood up straight, dramatically raising a fist to his heart as he proclaimed. "I apologize too. I pledge that we will hunt the perpetrator down and deal with him as you desire."

Rafe frowned at the ostentatious show the

Enforcer put on, especially when he snuck a glance his way and smirked. What he wouldn't do to wipe that damn smug look off his face.

"Excuse me?" Tasha tugged on Zohar's arm. "Did I hear correct? I can decide what happens to this person when we catch him?"

Zohar turned his full attention back to Tasha, that smug look gone as he smiled down at her upturned face. "Of course. It is your Pack that has been destroyed. It's only fitting you decide the punishment."

Rafe watched as a host of emotion flashed across Tasha's face. Excitement was first, then worry, hurt, and last of all was resignation. She'd made up her mind and it didn't take long for them to find out what she'd decided.

"Death by Wolves. Seems fitting after what they've done."

"Then we'll do our best to honor your wishes." Zohar saluted her, his huge body towering over her.

The sight making Rafe uneasy enough that he stepped closer to his mate, snaking an arm around her waist and holding her against him securely. She looked up, a look of fiery determination on her face. Pride surged up inside him as he gazed down at her beauty and strength. She was already turning into a tough Alpha, one he was honored to have at his side.

Reaching up he ran a finger along her jaw, smiling down at her. "You're amazing, sweetheart."

"I am?" she asked, wide-eyed and confused.

"Yes, and you don't even know it, that's what makes it all the more so."

"Can we get this show on the road?" Zohar asked sarcastically, breaking the moment, pissing Rafe off again.

"Rafe, we're ready," Jacy said, surprising Rafe. He hadn't heard his Beta arrive. Looking around he saw the rest of his men waiting a few feet away.

"Okay, big shot, how do we go after this maniac and not get our asses fried by his magic?"

Zohar quirked an eyebrow toward Rafe before answering. "I have someone waiting on the other side of camp. He's set up and already got some spell or other in place. Apparently it should lead us to whoever it was that made the Pack sick."

The Enforcer stopped, staring hard at Rafe. "The information you managed to get out of that rogue you caught, he *did* say they were working for whoever it was that did that. Right?"

"Yes," Rafe ground out, remembering how the

rogue had almost taken Tasha from him. One slip of his wrist and the knife in his hand would've slit her throat.

That wasn't something he could dwell on or it would drive him insane.

Right now he needed his wits about him as he tuned back into Zohar barking orders. The Council's men scurrying about to do his bidding. Jacy and Levi waiting for Rafe's. "Get the vehicles and meet us on the other side of the camp."

Myrtle sped away after Jacy, her obvious unease at being anywhere near Zohar palpable in the air. He couldn't blame the girl. Zohar was cold, hard, intimidating and dangerous. He also had a short fuse and it was that point that always confused Rafe as to how the Enforcer still managed to rise up the ranks within the Council.

There was no doubt that the man got the job done, but at what cost? He would step on anyone in his path and to hell with it. Nobody was allowed to get in his way and that included innocents, like Myrtle. There was no need to insult and bully people to get what you wanted. But, Zohar didn't seem to follow the same rules as everyone else, and Rafe never let him forget it, or failed to stand up to the man when he felt the need.

He felt lucky that he didn't cross paths with Zohar too often. If he did, then he'd be forever bruised and battered, as would be the Enforcer.

"Rafe." Tasha tugged on his sleeve pulling him out of his thoughts. "Come on."

He noticed they were alone, Zohar and his men walking away quickly. Grabbing her hand and jogging to catch up. Their feet slapping against the soft grass, a fresh breeze cooling their skin against the heat of the sun. It would soon be hot-as-hades so it was just as well the corpses had already been dealt with. He dreaded to think of the stench if they'd been any later.

He vowed to come back and plant a crop of wildflowers over the mass grave and some sort of headstone to mark the place where an entire Pack lay. That was something that couldn't be ignored, they needed a memorial and he'd make sure one was provided.

Catching up to Zohar beside a large black SUV, they saw a small man sitting, arms crossed, head back and looking as if he were napping. He certainly didn't look like much but if the Council were confident in his magical abilities then Rafe would need to accept it. He just hoped the man's power far outweighed his diminutive size.

"Follow us," Zohar ordered, climbing up into the front passenger seat and slamming the door.

Jacy shouted them over and they got in the back of Rafe's Jeep. The first thing he did as he shut the door was ask his Beta "Is Myrtle all right?"

"She seemed a little shaken up." Jacy made eye contact in the rear-view mirror. "But we both know Zohar has that effect on most people. Don't we?"

"He's a bully."

"He can be, that's for sure." Jacy agreed before they settled into silence, following the long line of vehicles filled with Wolves sent from the Council.

How long would it take to find who they were looking for? He hoped it wouldn't be too long. His nerves were frayed thinking of Tasha being anywhere near the maniac that was powerful enough to take out an entire Pack. His stomach clenched, fear lapping at his belly, a loud cracking sound alerting him to the fact he'd demolished the handle on the door.

"You okay back there?" Jacy asked quickly glancing over his shoulder.

Tasha reaching over to snatch his hand away

from the mangled plastic in his hand. "I'll be all right. I promise to stay right beside you."

Her insight to what was wrong with him endeared her even more to his heart. Then she unbuckled her belt, slipping onto his lap and burrowing her head into his shoulder. She didn't say a word, just sat there, his arms around her holding her close. Her scent invading his senses and calming him, man and beast.

Nuzzling his nose into her silky soft hair he allowed his mate's presence to still his stormy waters. Her soft curves against his hard torso, her breath caressing across his neck, her fingers stroking his chest, all came together to fill him with such peace and joy. And other emotions hard on their heels: need, want, and lust.

His heart sped up so he could feel the vein in his neck throb, his cock hardening in his jeans to rub against her ass, and then Tasha felt it too. What did she do? Wiggled that delectably fine ass and peek up at him with a mischievous smile. If that wasn't enough, her tongue darted out to slowly lick along her bottom lip.

Damn! He was ready to throw her on the seat and tear her clothes off. The look in her eyes changed from playful to "oh hell" in a split second. She sat up, blushing scarlet, whispering, "Sorry, I've no idea what came over me."

Rafe exhaled, holding Tasha in place when she tried to escape onto the seat, her embarrassment flowing from her to surround him in a cloud. "It's okay, darling. It's our bond calling to us. We started our mating but we didn't exactly 'seal the deal' and both of our beasts are getting impatient. We'll be all right once we . . ."

Jacy interrupted indignantly. "Hey! I'm right here! I don't need to hear this stuff. Jeez, just get a room you two and be done with it."

"I would if I damn well could," Rafe groaned.

Tasha buried her face against his chest, mumbling, "Kill me now."

"Bit drastic, honey." Rafe laughed, settling down to continue the journey. With her in his arms he wasn't on edge, well, not as much.

On and on the journey dragged, sun beating through the windows, Jacy using the AC to keep them cool. Wolves bodies ran hot, so they were all suffering, apart from Tasha who was fast asleep in Rafe's arms. The heat from her body enhancing her scent, enveloping him in her aroma and soothing his soul.

“Damn it, how much longer.” Jacy shook his head, annoyance dripping from every word. “It’s been hours, Rafe.”

“We have no idea how far this guy had gone. He could be anywhere.”

Rafe felt the tension in his Beta as he concentrated on the road ahead. Yet another backroad, one of a dozen they’d driven along and not easy to navigate in the waning light. At least they didn’t need the AC anymore.

Not once had they gone anywhere near the interstate. No, this guy they were hunting had stayed away from civilization and main roads. Why? Rafe wasn’t sure but it made him uneasy. He had the feeling their prey was exactly where he wanted to be and they were driving straight into a trap.

Chapter 13

Rafe lurched forward, holding tight to Tasha to stop her from tumbling off his lap as Jacy stamped on the brakes. "What the fuck, Jace?"

"What's going on?" Tasha mumbled sleepily.

"Sorry," Jacy threw over his shoulder. "They just stopped dead with no warning."

Rafe shuffled Tasha onto the seat, struggling to open his door because of the mangled handle, giving up and opening the window, reaching out and opening it from the outside. "Stay here and I'll see what's going on."

"Wait." Tasha tried to scramble out but he quickly shut the door, leaning in the window to place a kiss on her nose.

"I won't be long."

Jogging along the side of the vehicles he had to

wind in and out of bodies too, many of the men exiting to see what the hold-up was. Nearing the lead of their convoy he saw Zohar lit up by headlights, fists on his waist as the small man Rafe had seen earlier spoke animatedly up at the large Enforcer.

"I tell you he is up ahead but there are magical traps set. If you go any further using these vehicles then you will be in danger."

The Witch's voice was high-pitched, more suited to a woman than a man, his head tilted back so he could glare up at Zohar. His body language screaming out that he was "in charge" and definitely not used to being questioned. With the power that Rafe could feel rolling from the diminutive man he wasn't surprised.

"What's up?" Rafe asked, slowing to a stop beside them.

"This, this . . . buffoon won't listen to me." The Witch glowered at Zohar, tapping a foot furiously.

"I don't see what difference it makes." Zohar waved his arms around him. "Carrying on in our vehicles or walking in. I'd say we'd be more in danger on foot."

"You,"—the Witch prodded Zohar's chest—"are an Enforcer, I am the Witch. Who knows best about magic? Hmm? You or me?"

Rafe grinned at the man's bravery as he stood up to Zohar. The man's black hair flying around his head as he swung it between the Enforcer then Rafe and back again. Rafe stuck his hand out, trying to defuse the growing anger. "Hi, I'm Rafe and you are?"

The Witch stopped his tirade, his blue eyes surprised as he looked up at Rafe who grinned down at him. "Oh, hello, I'm Sherman Kelly."

"Nice to meet you, Sherman. Now what seems to be the problem?"

Sherman took a deep breath in, held it for a moment then released it slowly, calming himself. "There are spells on the road. The person we are after is ahead and he's placed these for several reasons, the first of which is to stop anyone driving along here getting to him. The second is that any vehicles that proceed will then set off alarms that will give him the opportunity to escape, but that's not the main issue."

Rafe saw Sherman throw Zohar a stinking-filthy look before he continued. "Anyone *within* those vehicles will be, at best, knocked unconscious but I suspect the effects of the spell could have far worse consequences."

Zohar threw up his hands, exclaiming, "Well why the hell didn't you just *say* that?"

"Because you wouldn't listen!"

"All right, you two, stop it. Either that or get a room 'cause you sound like you've been married for twenty years." Rafe shook his head before turning to Sherman. "So what's the solution?"

"This Witch is powerful, but he has a fundamental flaw," Sherman said, tapping his nose conspiratorially. "He's lazy. He's placed his magic on the road and for a few feet either side of the road but that's all. There is nothing further afield so if we leave the vehicles here and go in on foot, giving the road a wide berth, we'll be fine. Well, until we reach him that is. Then the fireworks will begin."

Sherman finished with a flourish, clapping his hands and a distinct twinkle in his eyes. Rafe liked him. "Sounds like a plan to me."

Zohar didn't respond directly, instead he turned to one of his men, barking out orders. "Tell everyone to get out and onto the side of the road. They're to follow us precisely, no deviations whatsoever."

Rafe patted Sherman's shoulder. "I'll go and get my own men then I'll catch up with you."

"Fine, fine, just remember to leave this rascal

for me to deal with."

"Sure," Rafe replied, taking the opportunity he leaned down. "About that, if at all possible can you soften him up enough for me and my Wolves to deal with him? It's just that the Pack that he killed, you know, the *entire* Pack of Wolves that we buried? Well those were my mate's people and she'd like him to be dealt with Wolf style. If that's something you can do, Sherman?"

Sherman twiddled his fingers and leaned toward Rafe as he tapped the side of his nose. "I get you, Rafe. That bastard deserves all he gets and your lovely lady, well, I can't even begin to know how she must be feeling. If that's what she wants then I'll do whatever I can to make it happen. No promises, of course, because I don't know exactly what we're walking into, but if this lame ass spell he's got going on here is anything to go by then I feel confident that I can deliver him up on a platter to you. After that you can do what you wish with him and good riddance is what I say."

Rafe grinned, then winked at the Witch. "Thanks, I really appreciate that."

He took off, running back through the throng of bodies that now barred his way.

Annoyance at being held up by Zohar's men, he finally reached Jacy and Tasha, finding the rest of his men waiting too. His Beta pacing back and forth muttering under his breath. When he saw Rafe he relaxed. "Thank goodness! I thought you'd pulled a fast one and left us behind."

His hand flew to his mouth, eyes wide as he looked around. "Shit, I said that aloud didn't I?"

Tasha laughed. "Yeah, you did, but it's what we were *all* thinking."

"What?" Rafe sidled up to his mate, chucking her under the chin. "You really thought I'd do that?"

"Yes, no, not really," she mumbled, refusing to look him in the eye.

"I admit the thought crossed my mind but I gave you my word and I don't break that, Tasha. Not if I can help it."

"Sorry," she said, raising her eyes to meet his. "I can feel your reluctance about having me here so I thought you'd maybe taken the opportunity to leave me behind."

"I don't like that you're here but you are. It is what it is but my men all know they're to keep you safe at all costs. I trust them so let's get moving."

Rafe looked around, spying Myrtle. "Stay

close, Myrtle. I might need you."

Tasha nodded giving him a tight smile before he wrapped her small hand in his, tugging her along as he jogged back toward Zohar and Sherman. The Council's men heeding what they'd been ordered and staying well away from the road, spreading out into the trees that ran alongside. They moved quietly, with stealth and purpose, Rafe and his men reaching Sherman quickly.

The diminutive man strode purposely forward, his fingers intertwined across his chest and muttering low with words that Rafe couldn't understand. He whispered to Myrtle behind him, "What's he doing?"

She shook her head and shrugged. "Magic but it's far beyond anything I know."

So much for having his own Witch. He couldn't be annoyed at her though. She was more Wolf than Witch and never hid the fact she never courted the power her mother wielded. Myrtle was happier healing than anything else and focused any magical abilities in those directions. Rarely did she use her Witch side in anger, although it had been known.

A smirk slid across his face as he recalled a time when she'd come across a young Wolf bullying some pups. She'd lit his hair up, sending streaks of sparks to give him a jolt or two, not enough to do any real damage. It was enough to scare the hell out of him and when his parents came to complain, Rafe growled that they were lucky it wasn't him who had caught their son, and if they didn't get the little shit under control, then he'd do it for them. That soon shut them up.

His nose twitched, jolting him out of the memory, alerting him to a change around them. What the hell was it? Inhaling deeply he almost gagged on a scent he'd never encountered before. Foul, definitely, but it was more than that. It was almost as if it were alive, sliding over his skin and seeping inside. Shivering involuntarily as the malevolent force passed over him a second before Sherman's hand shot up halting them.

It wasn't just Rafe that was affected. Everyone that was in front, or in line with him, shook their heads, or swiped at their arms as if trying to wipe something away. He reached behind him, pushing Tasha back. "Stay behind me."

"Hold up, guys." Sherman shook his head. "Crafty so and so. I'll get rid of this in just a moment."

Zohar snarled, shaking his head violently as if a bee had made its way inside, swiping at his ear. Rafe fought to still his own hands from scratching at the skin on his neck. The feeling of a snake slithering around it and winding tightly to cut off his air. He knew there was no such thing but the feeling was there just the same. His beast howled in his head, pawing at the ground, desperate to be free to attack the non-existent threat.

Barely containing his shift as Sherman babbled words that held no meaning, his arms flying skywards and a moment later the sensations dissipated. Collective sighs of relief rang out all around, Rafe's included.

"Looks like he doesn't want visitors." Sherman chuckled.

"No shit," Zohar grumbled as they trudged on. "Can you tell how far away he is now?"

"Close, that's all I can say." Sherman shrugged. "There's no magic nearby so you can send a scout ahead if you wish but I'd urge caution."

Zohar pointed to the man nearest him. "Take one of your best men and go ahead. See if you can locate any kind of house, cabin, anything that this fucker could be holed up in. If you see anything at all, get your asses back here and let us know. Go."

Tasha's hand grabbed Rafe's, holding on tight. "What *was* that?"

"Hell if I know, obviously magic." Rafe saw her worried face upturned in the moonlight. Her pale grey eyes wide, darting side to side as if she expected an attack at any moment.

"What if he has rogues?"

"We have more than enough men here to deal with his damn rogues." He ground out through clenched teeth. In fact, he was counting on it. A day cooped up in the jeep had him ready to let off some steam and there was no better way than ripping into some rogues. The only drawback was having Tasha here. He couldn't allow her to be hurt.

Stomach clenching, roiling as if he was going to puke with the mere thought. Shit. Could he talk her into going back?

"Uh uh, don't say it." She shook her head. "I'm not going anywhere."

Damn. She was getting good at reading him already.

Her face fierce, cheeks flushed, one hand on her hip as she glowered up at him. She was beautiful and she was his. Pity she was stubborn too.

"Tasha . . ."

Her hand shot up, waggling a finger. "I said . . . don't say it. I'm not arguing with you. I am going to find this, this . . . *person* . . . who killed *my* parents and my Pack and I'm going to watch as he meets his end. Understand?"

His mind raced to come up with words to change her mind. He was Alpha. He always knew what to say to get his way but somehow, this time, words failed him. He was still going to try though, that was until they were rudely interrupted.

"Excuse me, but if you two lovebirds have stopped having a domestic then can we get going?" Zohar's tone dripped with sarcasm.

Rafe's eyes spun to spear him with a deadly stare. "Butt out."

"I would, but we're on a mission and I don't usually have to take part in marriage counselling." The Enforcer smirked, looking at Tasha then back at Rafe. "But I have to say, if you two are starting off like this then it doesn't bode well for your future. Hey, just saying."

Rafe strode forward, closing the distance between them, his lips curled back in a snarl. "Don't. Don't say, don't speak, don't fucking comment.

Tasha is off limits to you. You're a Neanderthal that's not much more than brawn with not a lot of brains. If you did have brains you'd have your own damn Pack, Zohar. You know it, I know it, everyone fucking knows it."

Zohar let out a growl, showing his teeth, his fists clenching at his sides. Rafe knew how this went. As it always did. The Enforcer would lose his temper and they'd be embroiled in a down and dirty fight in no time. Well, that's how it usually went. This time Tasha pushed her way between them, punching each of their chests as she went. She didn't hold back either, her face red with fury as she spat out.

"Stop it! You two are like a couple of teenagers having a pissing contest. We're here to find the person responsible for murdering *my* parents. So, can we go do *that*?"

Her words, tone, outraged face were like Rafe had been thrown in an icy lake. His heart dropped like a stone, aching for adding to her already immense hurt and anguish. Zohar seemed to fare no better, his eyes dropping to the ground, refusing to meet Tasha's.

"Come on," Tasha said coldly, spinning away and following behind Sherman who was already walking away.

Her back rigid, head high, every muscle screaming her annoyance. Rafe sighed, she'd never looked so magnificent as he jogged after her. Jacy joined him, slapping his back. "Hey, you and Zohar really need to stop this nonsense. I know he's a bit of a . . ."—his Beta stopped, glancing to check where the Enforcer was before continuing—"ass but you know that so why do you let him get to you? You're better than that, Rafe."

"I guess he just knows which buttons to press with me." Rafe admitted to his best friend something he'd never do to anyone else.

"Ya think?" Jacy chuckled.

Catching up to Tasha he remained silent, simply grasping her hand and slowing to walk beside her. She glanced up, her eyebrow raising briefly before she relented and her lips tugged up slightly, as they walked on quietly.

Taking in the area around them, long grass, trees, sounds of wildlife, large and small. The place would be beautiful if not for the reason they were there. Soft footfalls heading their way, he reached forward, halting Sherman, a finger to his lips.

Moments later Zohar's men ran into view,

sliding to a stop, standing to attention before their commander as he barked, "Report."

"Small house ahead with a contingent of rogues guarding it. We had eyes on a dozen but there are probably more inside. There's also a cabin off to the side with lights on, so it's safe to assume there's rogues in there too but there can't be many because of its size."

Zohar nodded, dismissing them before giving out orders to several of his men, dividing them into groups to surround the main house and cabin. "My men will take care of the rogues. Sherman, you'll stay with me and deal with the Witch. Rafe, you and your men can accompany us and take care of any stragglers inside the main house."

"Fine," Rafe agreed before looking for Levi to give out his own commands. "Levi, stay back with Tasha. Keep half a dozen of our men with you in case of any trouble."

Tasha opened her mouth to argue but this time Rafe would hear none of it. "No. You will not be involved in the breach. After the rogues have been taken out and Sherman has done his thing with the Witch, then, and only then, can Levi bring you in. That is not open for discussion."

She crossed her arms, glaring at him, her voice saying one thing as her body said another. “Fine.”

Zohar’s men started to break away in groups, finally the Enforcer turned to Rafe. “Let’s roll and put this fucker down.”

“Sounds good to me.” Rafe snarled as his Wolves followed, ready to tear apart some rogues.

Chapter 14

His beast champing at the bit to be released, he fought to contain it, his skin rippling with hair already sprouting through. Gritting his teeth, he forced his change down, allowing it to simmer just beneath the surface in case he needed to call on his Wolf quickly.

His long legs powering across the ground, thigh muscles tightening as he ran, anticipation rushing through him as their quarry was finally within their grasp. He only hoped his mate would get her wish and the death of the Witch would grant her some closure. Rafe also hoped he'd be the one to deliver the death blow to the asshole.

As they neared the Witch's hideout, sounds of

battling Wolves erupted in the night air, not surprising as Zohar's men had gone ahead to clear the way. What did surprise Rafe was Sherman. Somehow the small, rotund man had kept pace with them. How he'd managed that feat was beyond him, but he had, and the Witch didn't even seem out of breath. Maybe he'd used magic. No matter.

What did matter was that Sherman was right there with them as they raced through the final brush into a wide open area. Zohar's men cleared the way, with more than a few dead rogues littering the ground. Rafe's eyes spun around, taking everything in. The cabin off to the side had also been breached. The door hanging off its hinges, blood and bodies clearly visible.

Zohar's Wolves were good. It had only been minutes, but they'd attacked and killed the opposition quickly and efficiently. It looked like this was going just the way they'd planned. Rafe grinned as they slowed to a walk, closing in on the main house.

And that's when things went to hell in a fucking handbasket. He'd never been so damn grateful that he'd put his foot down and forced Tasha to stay behind because right now they were all in a heap load of shit.

The door to the house came flying off, yes, flying as in off the hinges and up into the air. It rose about twenty feet, at what appeared supersonic speed then crashed into a group of Zohar's men. Some in human form and a few in Wolf form, howls and yells rising in the night air as the solid oak knocked them for six. The sound of broken bones and the scent of blood rising around them.

Shit. One guy's head lay at a godawful angle. He was definitely not getting up again. Not in this life anyway. Zohar slid to a stop, Rafe barely stopping himself barreling into him as Sherman cursed loudly.

"What the fuck?"

Rafe kept his eyes on the gaping hole where the door used to be, a dark figure emerging, bathed in a blue light. "Shit," he mumbled at the sight.

The man who had appeared seemed to be floating, his hair sticking out all around, crackles of lightning sparking from the ends of his dark hair and his outstretched hands. His face looked stranger still. Eyes wild, mouth open with that weird blue light visible inside, all the way down his throat. Jeez, it was like a vision from a horror movie. One he didn't want to be witnessing in real life.

Magic. Rafe freaking hated magic.

Sherman stepped forward, shaking his head and muttering. "Theatrics, why do they always go for theatrics. Amateur."

Rafe looked at the small man, then at the dreadful vision descending toward them. Sherman had balls of steel in his opinion.

"I'll give you one choice." Sherman raised his voice to be heard over the noise of the crackling electricity. "Cut the crap or suffer the consequences."

Rafe stifled a chuckle. It wasn't exactly what he expected Sherman to say. Watching intently as the man they'd come for lowered to the ground but otherwise nothing else changed. Rafe kept his eyes glued to the sparking electricity, feeling waves of energy wafting toward him.

Sherman sighed. "So be it."

The next second a bolt of energy flew toward them from the man they'd hunted down, Rafe dropped to the ground but Zohar was a split second too late. He was blasted in the chest, lifted up off his feet and flown backward to land on his ass. He then tumbled head over heels to land with a loud gasp as the air was knocked out of him before he sat up, dusting himself off and snarling. Zohar sprang to his feet and rushed forward but Sherman shook his head, warning him not to go any closer. The Enforcer did not look happy.

"You all right?" Rafe asked, trying not to grin. Admittedly he didn't try too hard.

Zohar didn't reply, merely grunted before he snarled at Sherman. "Can we deal with this asshole now? That is why you're here isn't it?"

Sherman glanced up, squinting. "Indeed, but I didn't see Rafe being knocked on his ass."

Zohar looked like he was about to explode, his face red, like one of those cartoon characters. All it needed was for steam to pour from his ears and he'd be all set.

"Right, let's strip you of those powers." Sherman almost sang as his hands seemed to dance in the air, strange words flying out his mouth. He reached inside his jacket, pulling out a small green silk pouch. Holding it with one hand, he quickly stuck two fingers in and out, pinching something or other between them, before the pouch disappeared. He spoke faster, hands moving together again, his feet moving toward his foe quickly.

Rafe followed, scared the smaller man was

putting himself in danger. Sherman stopped barely a few feet from the man, and this close, Rafe could see pure evil staring back at him. He couldn't wait to get his hands on this fuck.

Sherman continued his incantation, his voice rising to a crescendo before finally throwing whatever he held in his fingers into the much taller man's face. The result was startling and instant.

The figure was no longer threatening. All signs of the electrical power he'd wielded disappeared, leaving in its stead a man that looked angry, shocked, and scared. His dark eyes darted around, looking for a means to escape. Futile. Rafe's own men now circling around to block his way, some in Wolf form, snarling and snapping their jaws menacingly.

"What did you do to him?" Zohar asked Sherman.

Sherman turned away from their foe, whispering so low that only Wolf ears would hear. "I've bound his magic but it may only be temporary. I've no idea how long it will last. I could easily have killed him but I did say I would try to give the lady her chance to face the man that did carried out such a heinous act on her family and Pack."

"Thanks." Rafe inclined his head as the small

man spun back to the person who'd been such a frightening sight just moments earlier.

"What's your name?" Sherman asked quietly.

Dark eyes narrowed in on him, a defiant tone as he answered. "Paulo, Paulo Capaldi."

"Why?" Sherman tilted his head. "Why would you abuse your power to kill so many people? You annihilated an entire Pack of Wolves, for what?"

Paulo's eyes closed to slits. "Why? Because I could, that's why. I wanted their land. Not just theirs. I would've carried on, gained as much as possible and sold it to developers. Do you have any idea how much land like this sells for? I could've made a fortune and all I had to do was get rid of a few mangy Wolves."

Rafe's beast reared its head, a rumble in his chest gaining momentum to escape into a savage growl. His fangs descended, nicking his cheeks and lips, blood dripping down his chin to drop onto the ground. He refused to rein his Wolf in, allowing Paulo to catch a glimpse of the future that awaited him.

"Get that thing away from me!" Paulo whined at Sherman.

Tasha appeared, tears running down her

cheeks. "You killed my friends, my Pack, my mom and dad, just for money. What kind of person are you that you'd abuse a power the Goddess gave you like that?"

Rafe's anger grew. His mate's suffering clawing at his insides like molten lava. Her pain was his pain. He could feel it. Raw, aching, agony, anguish and sorrow. He almost crumpled to the ground with the weight of what she carried. His Tasha, his love, and she needed him.

His arms circled her, bringing her back against his chest, holding her tight as his Alpha power flowed into her. His strength ebbed from him, giving her what he could to help.

Paulo merely sneered at her, sealing his fate. "What kind of person am I? I'm strong and use what I have to actually do something not just prowl around and live like wild animals. You Wolves are barely a step up from dogs."

Tasha's body shuddered, shock reverberating through her as Paulo's venom rushed over them. Sherman stepping forward, patting her arm. "I apologize for this idiot, my dear."

Zohar appeared, grabbing Paulo roughly. "I've been sent by the Council and I am their Legal

Representative. It's my decision what happens to you and your sentence has already been determined."

"What? No! You have no right. I'm a Witch and I should be tried by my peers not by you." Paulo yelled, his face contorted with rage but also fear.

Sherman took over, his voice cold and hard. "I've got the relevant authority from the Witch Council to dole out some justice."

Paulo pounced on Sherman's words. "Yes, yes, of course. You're a Witch, you're the only one that should deal with me. Take me back to the Witch Council and let them administer my punishment."

Sherman wandered away, his face grim, thoughtful, as he paced back and forth. Every so often he'd stop and glance at Tasha, then Paulo, then return to pacing. Tasha's heart thundered in her chest, Rafe could hear it clearly, her hands now hanging onto his as he still held her close against him.

Rafe's Wolves were growing restless, prowling around Paulo, or pawing at the ground, desperate to sink their jaws into him and draw blood. His Alpha power the only thing holding them at bay. Levi and Jacy joined the circling Wolves, adding to Rafe's authority and keeping the Wolves in check, for which he was grateful. His focus was wavering between them and his mate so the added help would ensure his men didn't suddenly attack.

Not that the bastard didn't deserve it but when the time came that pleasure was going to be his. He hoped. He may be Alpha of his Pack but he held no jurisdiction here. All they could do was wait and see what Sherman decided.

Zohar caught Sherman's pacing bug, walking away for several yards then beginning his own version. However, the Enforcer's was more energetic, more a stomping, as he marched back and forth, glaring at Sherman then Paulo and back again. The former ignored him, the latter squirmed every time Zohar's eyes bored into him.

Everyone could see the decision weighed heavy on Sherman. He hadn't expected to be put in this position, and now that he was, the man obviously didn't know what to do. He was well aware what would happen if he handed Paulo over to Rafe and his Wolves.

As it turned out, Sherman didn't have to make the decision he was having difficulty with.

Rafe's focus was on Sherman when Tasha shouted. "Shit!"

Sherman yelled. "Get back!"

Zohar snarling as he turned toward them.

Rafe spun around to see the beginning of that dangerous blue light simmering in Paulo's eyes, a dangerous glint shining as he smirked, gathering his power to garner an assault. His focus on Tasha, his hatred showing clearly as his face contorted in a mask of revulsion, spitting out. "Dirty fucking Wolf!"

"Hell no." Rafe growled, releasing his beast.

Razor sharp fangs descended, claws erupting, fur sprouting through his skin, as he threw Tasha behind him and leapt forward, mid-change. Half man, half beast, he attacked the threat to his mate, teeth tearing, claws ripping, skin, gore, blood spraying all around until there was nothing left of Paulo but a tangled mess on the ground. His blood pooled around him, seeping into the dirt, the metallic aroma hanging heavy in the air.

Rafe felt the viscous crimson fluid all over him, his clothes in tatters as he snarled at the body. Rage rampaging through him at how close his mate came to danger. His head spun around looking for something else to tear apart, eyes wild and feral, his blood rushing through his system like a tsunami, blocking out all other sounds.

Soft fingers ran through fur on his half-formed torso causing him to jerk around, Tasha's pale grey eyes peered up at him. "It's all right, Rafe. We're safe now. Come back to me, please."

Her gentle tone soothed his beast and his soul. His Wolf retreating to leave him standing in his tattered clothes and Paulo's blood. "Are you okay? Fuck! Tasha, I was so scared he'd hurt you."

"I know but you stopped him," she paused, blushing, "my mate. Thank you."

He crushed her to his chest, the mere thought of her being injured taking his breath away. Then he remembered the state he was in and quickly stepped back. "Sorry, I'm a bit of a mess."

"I don't care." She returned to his embrace. "Now can we go home and finish what we started?"

Her words had his heart thudding in his chest, his soul soaring high as he nodded. His voice suddenly thick with emotion as he answered, "I'd love nothing more, sweetheart."

CHAPTER 15

Rafe changed clothes as soon as they got back to their vehicle, glad they'd brought backpacks in case they were away for longer than a day. Pity he'd have to wait until they got home to get the stench of blood off him.

At least their return journey was faster, Jacy using the on-board GPS to reach the nearest highway then flooring it to speed along the almost empty road. Tasha's head resting on Rafe's shoulder in the darkness, his arm around her shoulders, holding her securely against him. He could sense the change inside her. She was still shrouded in grief but there was a sense of peace that now settled inside her that relaxed his Wolf.

She was on the road to recovery, a long road no doubt, but she was now going forward, and he'd be with her every hard step of the way.

Jacy glanced over his shoulder from time to time but when he saw Tasha dozing he remained silent. Rafe wasn't sure he'd ever known his Beta to keep quiet for so long before. It must be some kind of record. Whatever it was Rafe was grateful, it allowed him to reflect on his mate and the changes it would bring not just to him personally but how it would enhance the Pack.

A mated Alpha was more stable, not prone to outbursts, violent or otherwise, which was always beneficial for a Pack. It also meant, usually, that pups would soon follow and cement the Alpha lineage. Another plus for the stability of the Pack.

All of that mattered, of course it did, but truth was, all he cared about right now was how she made him feel. Complete. Loved. His heart speeding up to thunder in his chest whenever he caught sight of her, when her scent wafted over him. When she spoke and her words made his skin goosebump with anticipation and desire. The thought of that first time she shuddered beneath him as she fell apart in his arms. Those were the most important things to him right now, nothing else.

"How long?" he whispered.

"Soon," Jacy replied, turning off the main road.

Rafe looking out the window and seeing his own land in the darkness. The glow of the clock on the dash showing it was almost four in the morning. Not long now until he held her naked body against his.

"Shit." He swore, pushing those thoughts away as his cock sprang to life.

"What's up?" Jacy stage-whispered over his shoulder.

"Nothing." He snapped before gently waking Tasha. "We're almost home."

"Are we? Jeez, I slept most of the way again. Didn't I?"

"Yes," he laughed. "It's okay, it's been a long day."

"I need a shower." She yawned, stretching her arms and pulling her top tight across her chest.

Damn! His cock twitched again. "Down boy." He told it firmly.

"What?" she asked, frowning.

"What?" he asked back, feigning ignorance.

"I can't believe the Pack is taken care of. That

Zohar guy certainly knows how to get things done."

Rafe growled, hating the sound of the Enforcer's name on Tasha's lips. "He has a lot of men at his disposal."

"Yeah, I guess." She conceded. "I liked Sherman, he's nice and funny."

"Me too." Rafe agreed. "I wonder if Myrtle would like to train with him?"

Tasha shook her head. "No, don't push her into that. She's not that comfortable with her magical side. If she wants to pursue it then she'll do it on her own. If you ask her she might think it's because *you* want her to and do it because her Alpha wants it."

Rafe didn't answer right away, letting Tasha's words sink in and also thinking of Myrtle. The girl was definitely a "pleaser". He could see her agreeing to do something if he asked her to, even if it was something she didn't want to. What he was surprised at was that Tasha had figured that out so quickly.

"You're right," he finally said. "I know that about Myrtle, but I'm not sure how you realized that so quickly."

"I can read people well, it's just something I do." Tasha shrugged. "I can usually size people up pretty dang fast and Myrtle was easy. She's someone who doesn't like to say no and she'd do anything for her Alpha. But that's not always a good thing. Like this magic stuff. It's not something she really wants to do and there's no point in making someone unhappy. Is there?"

Again she'd surprised him with her insight. Not only was she sexy as hell but she was sharp as a tack too. Tasha was going to make one hell of an asset. To him and to the Pack. The Goddess sure had made the right choice when she'd chosen them for each other.

"Thank you," he said, lifting his head to send a quick word of gratitude skyward.

"What are you doing?" Tasha poked him in the ribs.

"Just saying thanks to the Goddess for sending you to me. You're amazing, baby, utterly amazing."

She flushed scarlet, his Wolf eyes seeing it even in the darkened interior of the cab as she batted at his arm. "Shush."

She fingered the gold chain around her neck, opening the locket and showing it to him. "This is my mom and dad. She gave it to me a couple of years ago. It was hers, my grandmother gave it to my mom, and my mom changed the pictures and said I should have it. I'd like you to see how they looked."

Rafe looked at the tiny image, a strong tall, dark haired man standing behind a smaller fair haired woman, arms around her waist. The woman's head tilted upwards looking back at the man with a smile on her face and a twinkle in her eyes. It was obvious to anyone how much they were in love with each other.

"They look happy, and in love. Your mother is beautiful, Tasha, you obviously take after her."

Tasha smiled sadly. "Thanks, and yes, they meant the world to each other. She wouldn't have left him even if she could have."

"I can understand that," Rafe replied softly. "I could never leave you either."

Tasha looked up, her lips tugging up at the sides. "Me too."

Rafe leaned down, his lips caressing hers in a ghost of a kiss. A promise of things to come.

"We're home," Jacy said, interrupting, as he pulled to a stop in front of the Alpha cabin. "And not a moment too soon. I expected you two to start the mushy stuff any minute. I'm outta here. See you around . . . sometime. When you surface that is."

Jacy tugged open the door because Rafe had

broken the handle earlier in the day, laughing his head off.

"You cheeky . . ." Rafe stopped, there was no point in continuing as Jacy disappeared. Instead he got out, reaching in and offering Tasha a hand. "Come on, we'll go have a nice warm shower."

"Together?" she asked, eyebrow raised.

"Together sounds perfect." He grinned, helping her out and leading her inside.

His mom must have been in and left lights on for them, there was also a tantalizing aroma floating through from the kitchen. Rafe's stomach rumbled. "We can eat later." He smirked as he headed upstairs, his mate on his heels.

"Later is good."

As they reached the bedroom door he stopped, palming his forehead. "Shit! I didn't think earlier. What with everything going on. What about your things? We can go back tomorrow and get what you need, or want."

Tasha reached up, patting his cheek. "I asked Levi to get Myrtle to help him pack up some stuff from my bedroom. That's enough for now. We can go back in a few days and I'll sort through everything else. It's not just my stuff, Rafe. I'll need help in contacting any relatives of the rest of the Pack in case they want to come and claim anything. But that's not for today, or tomorrow. That can wait . . . until after we're mated."

"You're right. There's more to do than I first gave thought to, but I'll help. We'll all help."

"Thank you." She tilted her head. "Can we have that shower now?"

Rafe pulled her after him straight into the bathroom, picking her up and sitting her on the space between the two sinks before turning on the shower. When he returned he leaned in, eyes open, his lips covering hers in a soft kiss which quickly turned hot and heavy. Their tongues clashed, tangling together as their hands fought to release the other of their clothes. She groaned into his mouth when his hand cupped her breast, finger and thumb tweaking her nipple into a hard bud. Groaning louder when he released her lips to duck down and suck her bud into his mouth. His eyes lifting to watch her head fall back, her spine arching as she pushed her breast further into his mouth.

Rafe's fingers made quick work of undoing her jeans, sliding them down over her hips as she lifted her backside up so he could slip them off completely.

As soon as she was naked, his fingers massaged her inner thighs, spreading them apart and slowly, slowly making their way higher to caress her warm folds. Dipping one finger inside, her hands wound in his hair, grabbing on tight, gasping his name.

Her soft mewls had his cock pulsating with need, but he wouldn't take her for the first time here. No. Not like this. This, here and now, was just a taster of things to come. His thumb slid into her warm sheath, coating it with her juices before going in search of that most magical of places: her pleasure center.

Rafe left her breast when he found it, his eyes on her face as he circled her clit with his moist thumb. Eyes wide, mouth open, Tasha locked gazes with him. "Oh my god!"

Grinning he swirled faster, using more pressure until he saw the moment she was about to fall over. Her hands left his hair, falling behind her as she screamed his name, her body shuddering her release. He kept up his soft rubbing, milking her orgasm until she leaned forward, head on his chest, mumbling. "What about you? And we didn't mark each other?"

Rafe laughed, loudly. "Babe, that was just the start. We've got a long way to go."

"Holy shit, you're gonna kill me." She groaned as he picked her up and carried her to the shower.

After a long, hot, and very steamy shower they finally made it to the bed. A freshly made bed with nice clean bedding. His mom had definitely been in.

"Are you ready?" he asked thickly, full of emotion as the moment his life would change forever drew ever closer. His arms around his mate, fingers caressing her silky skin as he gazed into her upturned face.

"I am," Tasha whispered. "I'm lucky to have found you, Rafe. You're more than I could've wished for in a mate. More than I dreamed I would ever get and what you've done for me, for my Pack, well, thanks doesn't cover it but it's all I've got."

"No thanks are ever required between mates, Tasha." Rafe leaned in, teasing the side of her mouth with a kiss. "I'd do anything for you. Anything. I'd kill for you. I'd die for you. I'll cherish you. From now and forever."

Her eyes filled with tears at his words, but he swiped an errant one away. "No tears. You've made me the happiest Wolf alive, baby. Now we need to seal our bond. Bite hard, bite deep, and make me yours."

Settling his body over hers, she opened her thighs to allow him entry to her warm sheath. Rafe teased her entrance with the tip of his hardness, her eyes widening in annoyance as she bucked her hips upwards. Chuckling, he obliged, sliding inside quickly, her channel widening to accept him, tightening around his cock. Damn, she felt so good beneath him. He was sure he'd never be able to leave the bedroom again, content to stay right here with her in his arms.

"Kiss me," she purred, longing and desire thickening her voice.

Lowering his head his mouth covered hers in a scorching hot melding of their love. His hips rocking against her as he plunged in and out, her heart rate shooting up as she rose toward another orgasm. The time was near, for both of them, bodies slick with sweat, skin slapping on skin, movements now frenzied with lust.

Tearing his lips from her mouth, he wound his fingers in her hair, tilting her head to the side and tugging it toward his neck. At the same time his mouth sought that sweet spot of hers, his teeth grazing her skin where he'd marked her before. Tasha releasing her canines and scratching his skin almost caused him to spiral over the precipice into ecstasy, barely holding on as he released his own fangs.

Burying his cock deeper with each thrust, he opened his mouth and bit down, hard, jerking as Tasha mirrored him. Blood pooled in his mouth, sliding down his throat . . . a sense of utter euphoria engulfing his entire being until finally he saw her Wolf in his head gamboling with his: their mating bond was sealed.

Releasing his bite, he drove into her faster and faster, head falling back as a roar like no other tore from his throat. The roar of an Alpha claiming his mate. A roar that announced to the entire Pack that their mating was complete. A roar that proclaimed that Tasha was his and he was the happiest man, and Wolf, alive.

~~~

Sunbeams shone through the window, settling on the far corner of the room, telling Rafe it was early afternoon. They'd slept for hours. Stretching carefully so as not to wake Tasha, a poke in his ribs alerted him to his mistake. She hadn't been asleep at all.
~~~

"Hey, beautiful." He grinned down at her, no sign of sleep in her face. "How long have you been awake?"

"A while," she answered. "I've just been watching you sleep. You look so peaceful and like a boy when you're sleeping."

"A boy?" Rafe frowned. Nobody could mistake him for a boy.

"Well, you just look relaxed and, it's hard to describe, kinda young and innocent."

Rafe couldn't believe it. Young and innocent. Those were definitely not words anyone he knew would use to describe him. "I think you're mistaken. The only one young and innocent here is you."

Her face flushed before she waggled her eyebrows. "After last night I don't think I can ever be called innocent again."

Rafe chuckled, moving quickly to cover her body with his. "I love you, Tasha Montgomery. More than you'll ever know."

Her fingers reached up, running down the side of his face, sending every blood cell straight to his cock. "I love you too, Rafe Blackstone."

"Glad we got that out of the way." He dipped his head, caressing her shoulder with feather light kisses.

"Are you hungry? Can I fix us something?" She breathed heavily at his touch.

He looked deep into her eyes, his hunger shining brightly, his heart full of love and contentment as he proclaimed. "Yes, I'm hungry, but no longer for food. My hunger is now for you, my mate."

Author's Note

Thank you so much for reading the first book in this brand new series. I hope you enjoyed Rafe and Tasha's story as much as I did writing it. If you could spare a moment to leave a review, I would very much appreciate it. As an Indie Author we value each and every one, so I thank you in advance for taking the time to do so. Keep your eye's peeled for more in this series. All of which will be standalones with happily ever afters.

There will be other authors joining the world of A Wolf's Hunger, which I'm very excited about. I'd like to thank them for taking the time to write for the series and I just know you're going to love the new additions. Also huge thanks to the girls over at Sassy Queens of Design, Becca and Angel, for another gorgeous cover to add to my collection.

Once again a thank you to Tammy Payne for her eagle eye in proofreading for me. She catches things that others don't! I appreciate you very much, Tammy, and hope you'll continue to work with me on all my future stories. Also my editor, Missy, for helping me make my stories better after she's got her hands on them!

Have a look for my other books, details in following pages. My author Facebook page details are below, so come and join me for a chat and let me know what you thought of the book. Join the Sassy

Lassie's VIP Clan to get inside information, deals, sales, and special giveaways. You also get a bonus freebie in your welcome email.

Have a great day and remember, Embrace Your Weird.

Live, Love, Read!

AVA

A Wolf's Hunger Series

Kade: A K Michaels
Marrok: Julia Mills
Ax: Monica La Porta

Coming Soon!

Saint: Bella Roccaforte
Holt: Desiree A. Cox
Tatum: S Raven Storm

Other Work by Ava

Escape: A Vampire Blood Courtesans Romance

Welcome to the world of Blood Courtesans.

Where Vampires are real and blood is a commodity that can give me my means of escape.

Money. Freedom. Escape. That's my only reason for selling myself, body and blood, to Maxwell Steele, this cold and lethal being before me.

I'll go to any lengths to escape being a prisoner within a Wolf Pack, including offering myself as a Blood Courtesan to a powerful and deadly Vampire.

First I have to escape the Pack, and my Alpha father.

Will Maxwell be strong enough to protect me? I hope so: he's my last hope for freedom and to live life as I want. I pray I'll survive, and I pray I'll keep my soul intact.

My name is Flora and this is my story.

Guild of Dragon Warriors

Master of the Guild of Dragon Warriors, Jaxon is heading back to their sanctuary, exhausted and injured, after a battle that the human realm has never before encountered. Supernatural beings fighting against the Demon King for survival of not only them, but all of humanity.

It was horrendous, tortuous, and downright brutal. He and his fellow Dragons were lucky to escape with their lives and all he wants now is to reach home and recover, knowing it will take days for him to reach full fitness again.

When an urgent call for help reaches them, he has no option but to head out again and give the aid that he is sworn to deliver.

What he finds is a unique being that is under threat and he vows to ensure her safety. No matter the cost.

His Dragon Warriors rally round and they must fight to protect the female in dire need of their defense. But Jaxon is not quite prepared for the consequences of his mercy mission and must make a decision that he never thought possible.

Come and follow Jaxon and his Guild of Dragon Warriors in Book one of New York Times Bestselling Author, A K Michaels' brand new series.

The Black Rose Chronicles

The Black Rose is a highly trained assassin. She is

different, exceptional, and one of a kind. An anomaly, she knows she's the only Witch/Wolf hybrid left alive. Only two people know the truth about her: her father and her mentor; her savior, Seth. If anyone even suspected her secret, she would be hunted down, for her unique DNA is beyond value.

She is strong, fearless and powerful. Rose kills with impunity if the target deserves such a sentence. Unfortunately, far too many do in this lawless land filled with Shifters, Vampires, Demons and more. Her latest assignment has the most powerful Vampire in existence in her crosshairs, and don't forget the Demon with a hidden agenda. Can Rose decipher all of the deceit and lies and make the right decision? One that will literally save the world and all of its inhabitants. Human and Paranormal alike.

Book 1 in New York Times Bestselling Author, A K Michaels' award winning series filled with paranormal beings in abundance. Shifters, Vampires, Witches, and more are all in this contemporary fantasy story filled with thrills, excitement and Paranormal Romance.

Reviewers are calling it, "Captivating," "Beautifully written," and "A simply brilliant start to an incredible series."

Highland Wolf Clan Series

Read the book that has over 200 five star reviews! Reviewers are calling it "gripping," "suspenseful", with "lots of love and action" and a series "I couldn't put down"!

A man born to be Alpha that walks away from his birthright and Pack. Cameron Sinclair wants nothing to do with either.

When summoned he reluctantly goes to the aid of his Uncle's Pack. What he finds is danger, intrigue, heartache, and the chance of a different life.

His instinct screams at him to walk away but his heart has other ideas. Come and join the Highland Wolf Clan and find out what's in store for Cameron and his Highlanders.

The Witch, The Wolf and The Vampire Series

A witch on the run, hunted by her father...and pursued by two men who desperately want to make her theirs. You know what they say...what happens in Vegas, stays in Vegas.

Peri is haunted by memories of her father's dark, magical cult, who tortured and imprisoned her throughout her childhood. Even six years after her escape, Peri is still a wanted woman, and is only able to stay alive by tracking criminals as a bounty hunter, constantly on the move and always alone.

Her travels lead her to Las Vegas, where a job turns bad. Wounded, she collapses at the feet of a stunning, ancient vampire named Josef, and gorgeous wolf shifter Gabe. Josef and Gabe tend to Peri's injuries, both of them falling in love with her. Claimed by both the vampire and the werewolf, Peri is caught in the middle.

As the romance unravels, Peri discovers her magic is far more powerful than she realized. Yet her father is searching for her, and Peri doesn't know if she's strong enough to stop him from taking her back. Trapped in a complex love triangle, who will Peri choose? Josef? Gabe? Or perhaps…both?

A thrilling urban fantasy full of adventure and suspense, *The Witch, The Wolf and the Vampire* is an erotic paranormal romance with a throuple taking center stage. This magical dark fantasy will have readers swooning for the next book in A.K. Michaels supernatural science fiction series.

The Witch, The Wolf and The Vampire: Next Generation, A Son's Fate

A gripping addition to The Witch, The Wolf and The Vampire series by New York Times Bestselling Author, A K Michaels.

Follow Joey's journey as he says goodbye to his life of luxury, with doting parents, and a sister he loves in 'Sin City'. With each passing day he is more unsettled as his Wolf strives to live as its DNA is programmed: within a Pack. After all, it's not just any Pack he wants. He is determined to join the very Pack that almost killed his father. He has no idea of the hardships ahead, but he faces everything with a deep resolve to gain his dream: Alpha status. Nothing less will suffice, even if he dies trying. Joey will give up everything to win his rightful place and seal his fate.

Joey is certain he won't settle for that alone. No. He craves to be Alpha and he'll do whatever it takes to achieve his goal. Including deceiving his parents as he uses underground fighting clubs to toughen up.

After all, it's not just any Pack he wants. He is determined to join the very Pack that almost killed his father.

Supernatural Enforcement Bureau Series

As Director of the Supernatural Enforcement Bureau, powerful Vampire Ronan, thought he had seen it all...until he discovers that Dragons actually exist. Can he help the Dragon being hunted on his patch? He certainly has the means at his disposal...if they can find it first...before the dark magic-wielding Witches and their Vampire cohorts.

After seeing the magnificent beast with his own eyes he can't turn from the task, even if he wanted to. Especially as his Sire, Josef, gives him a direct command to find the Dragon and keep it safe. No matter the cost.

With rogue Vampires and Witches on its trail, it's only a matter of time before they capture it. That's not something Ronan will allow...not on his watch! He will do whatever it takes to find and save the Dragon, using every powerful being at his disposal, including the dark and dangerous Creed.

Sabrina's Vampire Series

Sabrina's life was a mess, suspended from her police job, she ran to Vegas for a break, to escape the torment and embarrassment. She followed this up by getting blind drunk and down an alleyway with two thugs who wanted more than a goodnight kiss.

Kyle, a Vampire, hears her scream and against his better judgement enters the alley and saves her. As she collapses into his arms he had a deep need to take her home? He never takes anyone to his home. Soon Sabrina is ingrained in him - he can't get enough - can't let her go and just why are his bites not healing on her neck? When he finds out he is shocked - he must keep her - make her stay.

Will she? Will this woman stay in the arms of a Vampire?

Defender's Blood Series

Alex has no idea her life is about to change beyond her wildest imaginings. She is the last in a long line of very special females born for a dangerous task, and she isn't sure she is up to it. Zach, her vampire protector, is just as sure she is.

Demon attacks, angels and even the ultimate, divine intervention, shake Alex to her very core. Can she do this? Can Zach keep her safe? The alternative is unthinkable: demons once more ruling the earth.

Zach has to ensure that Alex puts a stop to this - and quickly.

Lori's Wolf Pack

Lori's lost in the forest, regretting her idea to go for a hike. Hurt and getting more terrified by the minute, especially when she hears the howls of a large animal nearby. In her haste to get away she falls and knocks herself out.

The animal finds her, having heard her screams.

The Wolf changes and the Alpha looks down at the female. As soon as he picks her up, his body reacts and he, at first, has no idea why. All he knows is his Wolf wants out, wants to mark this human as his.

Lori is oblivious to what's in store over the next few days as the powerful Alpha carries her to his cabin.

Adult content in this novella, no cliffhanger, and a happy ever after.